CONTENTS

PART 1
Twisted Sister

Corkscrew Willow (*Salix matsudana*)

Deciduous – China – 16 metres

CHAPTER 1

The sun was in my eyes. I had to squint to see the new kid clinging on. He was high up among the branches of the tree we called *Twisted Sister*. It was a corkscrew willow tree and its name had been well chosen. It was a crooked and tangled maze of brown and green above me. The new kid had his arms wrapped around its trunk over halfway up.

Down on the ground, five of us had our necks cricked back to watch him climb. I stood next to Mish. She was wearing the leaf earrings I'd got her last Christmas and her favourite black T-shirt. She pushed up the fringe of her curly hair and held her hand like she was giving a salute, shading her eyes to see.

"I told you he was a good climber," Mish said. She'd been the one to call me and I'd raced to the park on my bike.

It was Friday afternoon. Zoe was there too, standing on the other side of the tree with her boyfriend Marvin and his twin brother Harvey. Zoe had told Mish at school that there was a new climber hanging around.

The five of us stared up at the new kid. He was at least seven metres above us. He sat on a branch with his legs dangling down each side. He looked out of breath to me. He looked stuck too. I didn't think he was going to make it any further.

"What's his name?" I asked Zoe.

"He said to call him *Nottingham*," she told me. "He said it's where he comes from and that's what everybody calls him."

Zoe was in the same class as me and Mish. Marvin and Harvey were in the year above us. Zoe was lanky, skinny and fearless. She was a better climber than her boyfriend and his brother put together. She was the only one out of those three who'd ever made it to the top of *Twisted Sister* before.

"How long's he been up there?" I asked.

"Not even ten minutes," Zoe replied. "He climbed two of the smaller trees first."

"He's fast," Marvin said.

"Real fast," Harvey agreed.

They might have been twins, but they were opposites in loads of ways. Harvey's brain was bigger than his muscles. He was the only person I'd ever met who got excited about taking exams and he often went into a sulk if he didn't get top marks. Marvin's muscles were bigger than his brain. He never got top marks in class but didn't really care. He was a short, chunky rugby player. When he held hands with Zoe, he looked like a brick that was in love with a golf club.

"Maybe this new kid's faster than you," Zoe said to me.

Mish glanced at me out of the corner of her eye.

I shrugged, not wanting to admit just how fast Nottingham must be if he'd already made it halfway up *Twisted Sister*. It wasn't the tallest tree in the park, but that didn't mean it was an easy climb. There were plenty of us who had tried and failed, tried and failed, tried and failed. And failing mostly meant falling.

We watched as Nottingham searched for a way up in the brown and green maze. He shuffled his backside this way and that. The branch beneath him shuddered. Flutters of leaves fell.

Nottingham was wearing a black baseball cap and a green sweatshirt. Both of these things were good for climbing. The cap helped keep flies out of your eyes – or falling bits of twig and bark dust. Green clothing stopped too many leaf stains from showing, and that meant parents wouldn't always spot how filthy you were when you went home. But Nottingham was also wearing cargo shorts and that was a big mistake. His shins and ankles could get ripped to shreds by thorns and jagged branches. Hungry insects could chow down like he was KFC. I wished I could see what kind of trainers he had on.

"I bet you he makes it," Marvin said. "All the way up."

Harvey nodded.

Mish looked at me to see if I agreed.

"He's the wrong side of the trunk," I said to Mish. But I spoke loudly so Zoe and the twins would hear too. "If he was on the other side of the trunk, he could go for better branches." I pointed

19/04/22

Leabharlann na Cabraí
Cabra Library
01-2228317

Young
Adult

the Climbers

KEITH GRAY

Barrington Stoke

For Clara, Marc and Ludwig –
cousins and friends

First published in 2021 in Great Britain by
Barrington Stoke Ltd
18 Walker Street, Edinburgh, EH3 7LP

www.barringtonstoke.co.uk

Text © 2021 Keith Gray

The moral right of Keith Gray to be identified as the author
of this work has been asserted in accordance with the
Copyright, Designs and Patents Act, 1988

All rights reserved. No part of this publication may be
reproduced in whole or in any part in any form without the
written permission of the publisher

A CIP catalogue record for this book is available
from the British Library upon request

ISBN: 978-1-78112-999-9

Printed by Hussar Books, Poland

to show where I meant. "See there? The branches on this side are too tight to climb in between."

I was the youngest climber ever to make it to the top of *Twisted Sister*. I'd done it last summer when I was fourteen. But I'd fallen seven times before I'd made it. Could New Kid Nottingham really reach the top in one go?

I hoped he fell.

CHAPTER 2

I'd read this book once which said corkscrew willows were Chinese trees. So how the hell one had ended up in our park in our village was anyone's guess. They were also sometimes called "tortured" willows because their branches looked like they were twisted up in agony. Without its leaves in winter, *Twisted Sister* looked like it was screaming. But in summer it was a lush green explosion.

I'd also read that they should only grow as high as ten or twelve metres. *Twisted Sister* clearly didn't give a damn about what a book said, as it stabbed the sky at sixteen metres tall.

There were two massive problems when trying to climb a corkscrew willow. The first was all those branches. You'd think a tree with so many branches would be easy to climb. But they were coiled and tangled together like wooden snakes. You had to squeeze in between the branches, but the gaps could be too narrow. You could get yourself trapped. We'd all heard the story about little Lola Jones from Year 7. Lola had got wedged in *Twisted Sister* so damn tight that her dad had had to fetch a ladder and a chainsaw. She'd never climbed again.

Looking up, I thought New Kid Nottingham had got himself stuck. Not trapped, just at a dead end in the towering maze. But he surprised me.

More leaves shook free as he got down flat on his belly, the branch underneath him bending, bending. He slid himself along the branch away from the trunk and squeezed under two curling branches that twisted over his head. It looked dangerous. He had to let go with both hands. But he could then reach out to grab the branches higher up. He wriggled and forced himself into the gap. No one had ever tried a move like that on *Twisted Sister* before.

The five of us watching below him were impressed. But I pretended not to be.

"He's going to make it," Harvey said. He was taking photos with his phone. "First try."

But, like I said, there were two massive problems when trying to climb a corkscrew willow. The second was that they grew fast. Too fast. It meant they didn't always grow *strong*. The bark would split and the branches could be brittle.

New Kid Nottingham had no idea he'd pulled himself onto a brittle branch. He was still on his belly and the branch below him bent too far. He was looking down at us head-first. His cap slipped off as he tried to clamber backwards. But the branch broke. We heard the *crack*, as loud as a gunshot in a movie. We heard Nottingham's yell as he fell.

He tumbled and bounced, branches thwacking him, whapping him. He grabbed at thin air. Bark cracked and leaves exploded. Nottingham yelped and swore and grunted. He came down fast.

We jumped backwards away from the tree.

Nottingham hit the ground with a thud.

The branch he'd snapped came down after him. He rolled to one side and the branch missed him by centimetres.

Harvey still had his phone out and I wondered if he was going to call an ambulance. He took more photos of Nottingham on the ground instead.

And Nottingham had been lucky anyway – he didn't need an ambulance. He moved like a creaky robot, but he managed to get to his feet. He was groaning and pulling faces like he'd just been in a fight and lost. To me he had. He'd been in a fight with *Twisted Sister.* I knew that if he lifted up his green sweatshirt, he'd be scratched and battered and have bruises blacker than bats' wings. Even so, he managed to grin at us all standing there.

We often told the same old joke to each other: "Who are the best climbers? The ones who bounce back." But it was more serious than funny.

Nottingham was a bit taller than me and had thicker shoulders too, stretching his sweatshirt tight. His hair was dark, short and messy. He had a round, flat face. I wondered if it was so flat because he landed on it every time he fell from a tree. Across his right cheek was a thin worm-like scar. It went from underneath his nose all the way to his ear. Maybe he'd been slashed by a sharp branch when he was younger? I couldn't decide if the scar made him look ugly or cool.

I also checked out his trainers. A pair of old-school Adidas Swift Runs that had once been white. They were the best climbing shoes because they were brilliant at jamming into small gaps with their narrow pointy toes that had extra grip. And the pair Nottingham was wearing looked exactly the same as the pair I had on.

Of course part of me was glad he'd fallen. But part of me felt guilty for feeling glad that he'd fallen.

Nottingham touched the top of his head, then looked all the way back up to the spot from where he'd just dropped and crashed.

"Bloody tree stole my cap," Nottingham said. It was true – his black baseball cap hung on a twig high up there.

"I'll get it for you," I said.

Nottingham frowned and got in between me and the tree. "It's my cap," he said. "Don't worry about it. I'll get it."

"I'm not worried," I said as I tried to push past him. "I can do it, easy."

He got chest to chest with me. "Who the hell are you?" he asked.

"I'm Sully," I said.

"OK, Sully, and why the hell d'you think I need your help?" he asked.

"Because I'm the best climber in the village," I said.

Nottingham looked me up and down, still frowning. But then he grinned.

"If you say so," he said.

He turned his back on me, stepped up to *Twisted Sister* and started climbing again.

CHAPTER 3

New Kid Nottingham had learned from his mistakes. He didn't get himself trapped on the wrong side of the trunk on his second climb. He went slower too. No showing off this time. Instead he looked three branches ahead, checking for the best handholds. He was like a chess player working out his best move.

"How many falls did you have before you got to the top?" I asked Zoe.

"Ten," she replied. "What about you?"

"Seven," I said. We called any failed attempt a "fall", even if you only got stuck and climbed back down safely.

"Twelve for me," Marvin said. "So far ..."

"I reckon this new kid's gonna make it after just one," Harvey said. "He's got monkey blood or something. Hey, Sully, you should challenge him to a competition."

"Yeah," Marvin agreed. "You should have a race up *Double Trunker*."

"Sully would win. Easy," Mish said, defending me.

"Maybe," Zoe said. "But this new kid's got *reach*. Look at him!"

We looked. Telling a climber they had *reach* was the biggest compliment you could give them. It was like telling an athlete they'd won an Olympic medal. But also like someone beautiful saying you were a good kisser.

We watched Nottingham pluck his cap from the end of the twig that had caught it. He waved the cap at us before putting it on again.

Harvey waved back. Then he began fiddling with his phone.

"Who're you texting?" Marvin asked him.

"Everyone!" Harvey said. "They've gotta come see this, right?"

I couldn't take my eyes off Nottingham. He let both feet dangle in thin air as he tested the strength of a branch above him. It must have felt safe, because he pulled himself up. Higher. He stepped around the trunk like he was on solid ground. He had no fear. He squirmed between the corkscrewing brown and green branches. Higher. Ten metres, twelve metres.

Other climbers arrived to watch. I knew them all. They were out of breath because they'd raced all the way here to see it. Some on foot and some on bikes like me. Soon there was a crowd of kids in green T-shirts and Swift Runs around the bottom of *Twisted Sister*. We all jostled to get a good view of Nottingham past the leaves and branches.

Marvin's mouth gaped wide. "He's only gone and done it," he said.

We were all amazed.

No one had ever climbed *Twisted Sister* after only one fall. None of the older kids. Not even the first climber who'd given the tree its name.

Nottingham swayed a bit as he clung to the thinnest branches at the very top of the tree. With the sun behind him he was just a dark patch among the leaves, but we could see him waving. The twins started clapping him and whooping, and others in the crowd joined in.

I stayed silent. Mish tried to squeeze my hand, but I wouldn't let her.

Zoe looked at me. "Admit it, Sully," she said. She pointed up at Nottingham. "Maybe you're not the best climber in the village any more."

PART 2
Spider Trap

Larch (*Larix decidua*)

Deciduous – Northern Hemisphere – 19 metres

CHAPTER 4

There were trees here, there and everywhere in our village. Maybe more trees than houses. And we climbed them all. But it was the ones in the park that were totally legendary. We called them the "Big Five".

The Big Five trees stood like guards along the back edge of the park, which was also the back edge of the village. Beyond the Big Five were just flat fields, going way off into the distance. The view from the top of the Big Five trees was stunning.

From shortest to tallest they were *Twisted Sister*, *Spider Trap*, *Crazy Ash Bastard* and *Double Trunker*.

But that was only four, right? That was because the biggest, tallest, most difficult tree to climb didn't have a name.

Not yet.

Around here we had a climbers' code. Everyone knew that whoever was the first to climb a tree got to name it. And so far no one had got to the top of the last of the Big Five.

Not yet.

The unnamed biggest of the Big Five stood in the furthest corner of the park, on the opposite side to the play area with its swings and slide. It was boss, chief, master, elder of all the trees. I reckoned the view from the top would be mind-blowing. This tree was so big and tall it was like a massive pin sticking the park in place. I sometimes imagined a giant coming along and yanking the tree out of the ground, and our village simply floating away.

I was the best climber in the village. Chris Sullivan, but my mates all called me Sully. I had *reach*. And I'd made up my mind that this summer I was going to be the first to climb the last of the Big Five.

I was going to conquer the unnamed tree. I'd be famous and remembered for ever because I'd choose its name.

I was going to call it *Sullivan's Skystabber*.

CHAPTER 5

I'd thought I was going to be the first to climb that biggest tree, but that was before I met Nottingham.

He made it back down to the ground after climbing *Twisted Sister*. I saw he had leaves and bark dust stuck to the sweat on his cheeks and forehead. The long thin scar on his face was shiny pink. I knew the palms of his hands would be scraped red and stinging. He probably had jagged splinters in his fingertips too. But Nottingham was grinning like he'd just saved a drowning puppy, or maybe defeated a raging dragon. You know, like he was a hero.

The problem was, everybody who'd crowded around the bottom of *Twisted Sister* acted like Nottingham really was a hero. They all wanted to tell him how great and brilliant and amazing he was. Harvey even slung his arm around Nottingham and took a selfie. Then everybody wanted a selfie with him. I felt myself getting pushed towards the back of the crowd as they elbowed me out of the way.

I tried to pretend I didn't care. But I cared so damn much! What if this new kid *was* a better climber than me?

I was shocked when I saw Mish also had her phone out. She was my best friend. We'd been friends since we were eight, when she hadn't grassed me up for stealing some stamps from the Post Office. So Mish wanting a selfie with Nottingham stabbed me like a million burning splinters. But instead she held her phone up above everyone's head.

"He's not as fast as Sully," Mish shouted. She pointed at her phone so the other climbers could see it. "I timed him. Nottingham took twenty-two minutes and forty seconds to make it to the top. See? Sully can make it up in twenty minutes flat."

Zoe rolled her eyes as if Mish was just being annoying. But Mish always stuck up for me. She wasn't a climber, but we said she was like my coach and my trainer. The best climber in the village needed a support crew, right?

"Good try," I said, feeling relieved. I pushed my way towards Nottingham past the small crowd of kids who were meant to be my friends, not his. "But some of the trees around here are real hard climbs. Maybe a lot harder than the trees where you come from. At least you got your cap back."

Nottingham squared up to me. "You've got a seriously big head on you," he said. "I suppose it needs to be big enough to fit your big mouth."

Some of the kids laughed, some gasped too. But I just shrugged. I'd heard it all before. I was often told I had a big head, that I was boastful and a show-off, or even that I was too big for my boots. Whatever. It didn't change anything. I was the best climber in the village: one hundred per cent I was. It wasn't boasting if all you were doing was telling the truth.

"What if I told you I'm the best climber where I come from?" Nottingham asked.

"There are a lot of trees in Nottingham, are there?" I asked. "In Nottingham *city*."

Some of the other climbers chuckled and I grinned at them, lapping it up.

But Nottingham nodded. "There are loads of trees just outside the *city*, yeah. You've never heard of Sherwood *Forest?*"

He laughed at the look on my face. I tried to hide how jealous I felt. I knew I'd love to climb in a forest. And Sherwood Forest was one of the most famous forests in the world. I reckoned the trees there would be amazing.

"I bet there are some brilliant trees in Sherwood Forest," Zoe said as if she could read my mind.

"Awesome trees," her boyfriend Marvin agreed.

"The best," his brother Harvey said.

Then all the other climbers were agreeing and asking Nottingham questions about the trees in Sherwood Forest. How tall were they? What kind of trees? How many had he climbed? Were they taller than the Big Five?

"I've not climbed them all," Nottingham said. "There are too many in the forest. But I bet I could climb any tree here."

I reckoned I wasn't the only one with a big head.

"I'll bet you," I said. And everyone went silent. "I bet I know a tree you can't climb."

I saw a flash of worry in his eyes. But he couldn't back down.

"Now?" Nottingham asked. "Right now after I just climbed this one?" He hooked a thumb backwards at *Twisted Sister*.

"No time limit," I said. "Go as slow as you like. Take all day for all I care. But straight up. No falls. Just one go. Deal?"

Nottingham looked more trapped here on the ground than he had been up there between the branches of *Twisted Sister*. The other climbers shouted for him to "*Do it!*" Everyone was excited for him to prove how good he was. He knew it was going to be more difficult to back down from my challenge than it was to climb down from a corkscrew willow.

"And if I make it to the top?" Nottingham asked. "What do I get if I win the bet?"

"You'll be the best climber in the village," Harvey yelled.

But I shook my head. No way.

"No," I said. "It takes a lot more than climbing just one or two trees to prove you're the best."

"How about you give him your bike, then?" Marvin said.

I was going to say no again, but the other kids were all nodding. All except Mish, who took hold of my arm and said it would be stupid to give him my bike.

Nottingham wandered over to the bikes lying in the grass. Harvey pointed out which one was mine.

"Don't agree to it," Mish said to me. "What would your mum say?"

Mum had given me the bike for my birthday last month. It had been the best present ever. I'd been out on it nearly every day since, escaping our house.

Nottingham nodded and rubbed his still-red palms together. "OK. Deal," he said. "It's a cool bike. I'll look good on it."

And then there was no way I could back down either.

We didn't shake hands. Instead we both spat on the ground at each other's feet to seal the deal.

"He's not going to win the bet," I told Mish, but maybe I was telling myself too. What was more important to me? Being called the best climber in the village or keeping my bike?

"Which tree?" Nottingham asked.

I reckoned the other climbers thought I was going to say he had to climb the biggest tree, the last tree, the one without a name. But I was worried about how good at climbing he was. And Nottingham naming that last tree would be worse than losing my title or my bike. So instead I pointed to the larch tree in the park's back corner. We called it *Spider Trap*.

"That one?" Nottingham asked. "You're kidding. Dead easy."

Nobody agreed with him.

CHAPTER 6

At least fifteen climbers followed me and
Nottingham across the park. This was exciting
entertainment. Almost as exciting as climbing a
tree for themselves. There were some noisy little
kids playing on the swings and slide, but they
were still too young to be good climbers. Even so,
I reckoned a few of them had already had a go at
Spider Trap. It looked so easy.

The larch tree had a spindly carroty shape
that went up to a point at nineteen metres tall.
It looked to be a doddle of a climb because of
its curved, sweeping branches. They seemed as
regular as ladder steps. It had tight clusters of
needles rather than leaves, but nothing a pair of
gloves couldn't handle. I reckoned Nottingham
was thinking I was crazy to choose such a dead
easy tree. I was worried someone might tell him
the real reason I'd chosen it, but everyone kept
their mouths shut.

Marvin wheeled my bike next to us as we walked. "I'll give it to whoever wins the bet," he said.

"Are you gonna climb too?" Zoe asked me.

I shook my head. "The bet is that Nottingham can't climb it. Everyone already knows I can."

"And you're not going to tell him to watch out?" she asked.

I shook my head again. "Why should I?"

"It's kind of mean," Zoe said. "Don't you think it's mean, Mish?"

Mish didn't answer. But I could read the expression on her face. And, yes, she did think I was being mean.

"I don't want to lose my bike," I said to Zoe.

"Do you care more about the bike or being the best climber?" Mish asked me.

Harvey was grinning, with his phone out ready for photos. He clearly thought it was going to be hilarious.

We all gathered around the bottom of *Spider Trap*. It was late afternoon, but the June sun still felt hot. The tree cast a splash of cool shadow.

"All I've got to do is get up, right?" Nottingham asked.

I nodded.

"No time limit and I get a nice new bike?" he checked.

I nodded again. I heard Mish tut.

Nottingham stepped up to the tree. The branches came down as low as his knees. I guessed he knew there was a catch or a trap. I just hoped he didn't work out what it was.

We gave our trees names for good reasons.

Nottingham took his black cap off. His spiky hair was damp and flattened underneath.

"Why don't you look after this for me?" he said as he gave the cap to me. "I won't be long."

"Keep it on," Zoe told Nottingham. "Seriously."

But Marvin shushed her. I reckoned he wanted my plan to work just as much as I did.

It seemed like all the other climbers crowded around were holding their breath. I was nervous watching Nottingham. I hadn't climbed this tree in ages and I hoped it still lived up to its reputation. Otherwise the bike would be long gone, with Nottingham's Swift Runs doing the pedalling.

Nottingham wasn't going to be rushed. He walked in a circle around the base of the tree, looking for the best branches to start. When he seemed sure of his choice, he said, "If you run off with your bike when I make it to the top, I'll find out where you live and kick the crap out of you."

"I won't," I said. But I realised I was hopping from foot to foot, feeling the tension in the air.

The larch's low branches swept out wide at the bottom of the tree. We all watched as Nottingham pushed between them to get to the trunk in the middle of all that spiky green. He put a foot on the lowest branch and stepped up, getting his hands on the trunk. Right away he stepped onto the next branch, both his feet now off the ground. Then he was fast up to the next branch, his head pushing up between the clusters of needles. Another fast step up.

Then he jumped down to the ground just as fast with a surprised yelp.

Nottingham swore and slapped himself on his face and neck.

He crashed his way back out from in between the branches. He tried to yell again, but he had a mouth full of cobwebs. I counted at least four spiders on his face and chin, with two more skittering around the back of his neck. One was stuck to the sweat on his cheek, its fat body pulsing and its long hairy legs waving. Nottingham flailed at himself, hitting himself, slapping himself. He danced around like he was banging his head to heavy metal music as he tried to get rid of the itchy critters in his hair.

Even if you weren't scared of spiders, shoving your face in a bunch of cobwebs would always be bad news. And *Spider Trap* had dozens and dozens and dozens of thick, sticky cobwebs hidden in its branches.

The crowd of climbers pointed and shrieked and howled with laughter. Everyone thought Nottingham's prancing and flapping and swearing was hilarious. He soon calmed down once he'd got over the disgusting surprise. But it wasn't only Harvey who'd had his phone out. The other climbers began flicking through their photos, laughing even harder. They'd be on Instagram, YouTube, TikTok in a few seconds. Nottingham would be a viral star any minute now.

"You tricked me," he said. He snatched his cap from me as I held it out to him. But before he put it back on again he brushed a hand through his hair in case there were any more bugs hiding in his fringe. He was angry and embarrassed and the thin scar across his cheek looked livid.

"You lost," I told him. "Fastest fall ever."

Mish took my bike back from Marvin with an overly polite "Thank you".

Nottingham clenched both fists, looking like he wanted to punch me. He had bright red bites on his face and forehead. I knew they'd break out in blobs as big as Smarties and be as itchy as hell.

"I'm a better climber and you know it," Nottingham said. "That's why you had to trick me. You know I can climb any tree here. All of them."

It was Zoe who pointed at the last of the Big Five, the unnamed tree. "How about that one?" she said. "It's the biggest in the village."

Nottingham acted like he wasn't impressed. "If you say so. No sweat. Seen a million of them in Sherwood Forest. Easy."

"No one's ever climbed it before," Marvin said.

Nottingham scoffed and looked at me. "Not even Mr Best-Climber-In-The-Village?"

Marvin shook his head. "No, but he says he's going to."

"It's the only tree around here that hasn't got a name yet," Harvey said. He was no longer interested in the photos on his phone. "Whoever climbs it first will get to call it what they want, just like with all the other trees." Harvey pointed at me. "He wants to call it *Sullivan's Skystabber*. At least that's what he tells everyone."

I was horrified by everything they were telling Nottingham and wanted them all to shut up. I glanced at Mish, but she just shrugged.

Nottingham looked disgusted. "That's the crappest, nerdiest name for a tree I've ever heard," he said, looking me right in the eye. Then he turned around and shouted, "Who wants to see me beat Sully to the top of this tree?"

Most of the climbers put up their hands and shouted, "Yes!" That hurt. They were meant to be my friends. Harvey had his hand up too.

"Meet me here on Sunday morning," Nottingham said to me. "Ten o'clock. No stupid tricks. Climber versus climber. Straight up. And when I beat you to the top, I'll give it a proper name."

"Like what?" Mish asked.

Nottingham looked across the park at the huge yew tree, the last of the Big Five. It towered over everything else at thirty metres high.

"I'm not gonna give it some stupid nerdy or fancy name," he said. "I'll call it exactly what it is: *King Big and Tall*."

PART 3
Crazy Ash Bastard

Ash (*Fraxinus excelsior*)

Deciduous – Europe – 23 metres

CHAPTER 7

Later that evening, Mish and I were in my bedroom. It was a mess. Mish didn't mind – she was used to it.

"Nobody wants someone from outside the village naming the last tree," I said. "It's our tree. Nottingham's only been here five minutes. He's not got *reach*."

"Can we just get this homework finished?" Mish asked. She pointed at the pile of French worksheets.

I didn't have a desk in my room and had to use the top of my chest of drawers to work on. Mish sat on the edge of my bed, trying but failing to get me to focus on our homework.

"It's Friday night," I said.

"Exactly," Mish said. "I don't want to leave it until the last minute on Sunday again. I always get bad marks when I rush my homework."

"You've been hanging around with brain-box Harvey too much."

She shrugged. "I just want to get it done."

But homework was the last worry on my mind. "*King Big and Tall* sounds like something a five year old would call the tree," I said. Again.

I couldn't sit still. I couldn't keep my voice down. I couldn't stop going on and on about Nottingham and our competition to climb the last tree on Sunday.

"I have to be the one to name it," I said. Again. "I've got to be."

With a growly sigh, Mish slammed her pen down on the top of my drawers. "I'm going home."

"What? Why?" I said.

"Because I want to get all this done," she said, slapping her palm on her French book. "We've got to hand it in next week. You said we'd do it together."

"I'm not any good at French," I said, pulling a face as if the French language left a bad taste in my mouth.

"Nor me," Mish said. "It's so difficult. Which is why I really, really need to try hard at it. But if you're not even going to bother ..."

"Why do you think Nottingham said to meet him on Sunday?" I asked. "Why not tomorrow? D'you reckon he's going to sneak back and try to climb the tree when I'm not there?"

Mish sighed again, but quieter. She gathered the schoolwork together and put it in her bag.

"He's so damn smug," I went on. "Not even from around here but reckons he's the best already. D'you think he's good looking?"

My question seemed to shock Mish. She gave me a weird look.

My question shocked me a bit too. "His scar's cool," I said, trying to explain myself. I ran my finger across my cheek, following the line of Nottingham's scar. "How d'you think he got it? I reckon a branch did it when he fell out of some tree in Sherwood Forest."

"I don't really care," Mish said. "I'm going. See you tomorrow."

"Don't go home," I said. "Let's go to the park in case he's climbing the last tree without me."

"It's nearly ten o'clock. He's not going to be climbing."

"Tomorrow morning, then," I said. "But early. First thing. In case he goes early too."

Mish shrugged. "Maybe. But I have to do this French. I hate being bottom of the class all the time."

More and more these days Mish was acting as if she didn't care so much about climbing. She didn't come out with me all the time like she used to. I'd thought it was because her mum had been ill for a while and Mish had to take loads of time off school to look after her. We'd all been worried that she might have to go into hospital. But even when her mum got better, Mish had stayed home more often. She'd told me she was still looking after her mum, but I began to think she was just catching up with all her schoolwork.

We used to meet up with other climbers under the trees at the side of the churchyard, or in the grove behind Cooper's Lot, or most often in the park. Mish would time me as I climbed, watching from below. She'd help me find the fastest routes and best branches. It was what we did. It was what most of the kids around here did. What else was there to do?

"You're not on Nottingham's side, are you?" I asked. "D'you want him to beat me?"

Mish was stepping over a pile of clothes on my floor and almost tripped with surprise. "What?"

"D'you fancy Nottingham and want him to beat me?" I asked.

"Don't be an idiot," Mish replied.

I shrugged. "You just said he was good looking."

"I never." She blushed, which made me instantly think she was guilty. "You were the one who said his scar looked cool," she said.

We stared at each other in silence, both waiting and worried about what was going to be said next. But then my brother barged in without knocking. I hadn't even known he was home.

"Hey, lovebirds!" Nev said. He was leering like a perv. "Hope you've both got your clothes on."

"Don't be a moron," I told him.

"Shut up, Nev," Mish said.

Nev made his eyes all big and googly, and laughed in my face. He had beer breath.

He was four years older than me with long greasy hair in a ponytail. He loved old-fashioned rock music, bands nobody normal had ever heard of. He'd been learning to play the guitar for about a million years. But since he'd lost his job as a forklift driver, he now spent most of his time in the local pub.

"It's about time you two got it on," Nev said. He stretched his lips in a beery, leery grin. "She's the only girl you're not scared of, isn't that right?" He pretended to punch me in the stomach. I curled up to protect myself and Nev slapped me hard around the head instead. I fell for it every time.

"Just tell me what you want," I said. "Then get out."

"Don't talk to me like that," Nev said. "I'm doing you a favour. One of your little mates is at the door."

Mish and I glanced at each other. Who'd be calling round my house at ten at night?

We had to push past Nev to get out of my bedroom. He slapped me again as I shoved by him and my eyes started to water.

"Answer the door yourself in the future," Nev said. "I'm not your servant."

Mish pretended not to see me scrub my eyes dry as we went downstairs. She was good like that.

It was still warm out and not quite fully dark yet. Harvey was waiting in my driveway with his phone in his hand. He seemed kind of excited, kind of nervous. He jittered on the spot. My first thought was that I didn't often see him without his twin brother. He was panting as if he'd been running.

"I've been trying to call you," Harvey said, waving his phone.

Our driveway was all cracked concrete and weeds. The fence running along one side leaned worse than the Tower of Pisa. Our car wasn't there, so I guessed Mum was still at work. She worked at the pub and probably had to send Nev home before he got too drunk.

"Why haven't you got your phone on?" Harvey asked. "I've been trying for ages and ages."

I did own a phone. But I hardly ever switched it on because a zombie had more life than the battery. I was embarrassed because it was so old and crappy – like everything of mine. Except my bike. The bike Mum had got me for my birthday was the newest thing I'd ever owned.

"He's stolen your bike," Harvey gasped. He shoved his phone in my face to show me some blurry photos. "Nottingham has. He's stolen your bike and hung it up at the top of *Crazy Ash Bastard*."

CHAPTER 8

I didn't believe Harvey at first. I really, really didn't *want* to believe him. But when I checked, my bike wasn't leaning up against the wall under the kitchen window where I'd left it earlier. And so I ran all the way to the park.

Mish ran with me. We left Harvey behind because he'd already run all the way to my house and was too knackered to run any more. I reckoned his massive brain was so heavy it weighed him down. He was always last in sports.

I was swearing as I ran. The park was only a few streets from my house and we didn't slow down once. I was swearing and telling Mish just how I wanted to kill Nottingham.

The park gates were closed, but we knew a gap in the hedge we could squeeze through. The play area was in darkness; the footy pitch was a silent open space under a small moon. We ran across the dry and lumpy grass and saw two figures standing in front of *Crazy Ash Bastard*. A golf club and a brick. Zoe and Marvin.

"Where is it?" I shouted at them. "What's he done to it? Where's my bike?"

They both pointed up into the tree.

I almost tripped over my own feet as I stared up into the tree's shadowy canopy. Over twenty metres up was my bike, moonlight glinting off the wheels and handlebars.

CHAPTER 9

"How?" I said, looking up at *Crazy Ash Bastard* and my bike. "How did he ...?" I could hardly speak. "How did he get it up ...? Up *there*?!"

"It's tied up with rope," Marvin said.

"You saw him?" Mish shouted. "And you didn't stop him?" She was as gobsmacked as me at what had happened.

Marvin shrugged. "Thought it was funny," he said.

"None of our business," Zoe added.

"I thought you were meant to be my friends," I said. "Not his."

And this time Marvin and Zoe both shrugged.

"At least Harvey told you about it," Marvin said. "Your bike might have been stuck up there all night otherwise."

"How the hell are we supposed to get it down?" Mish asked.

But I had a different question. "Where the hell is he? Where's Nottingham?"

Marvin and Zoe didn't know.

"He lives down Elmore Lane," Marvin said. "Maybe he's just gone home."

"I thought he lived on Ina Crescent," Zoe said.

The anger and stress was making my head boil. "So I can't even go get him to fetch my bike down if nobody knows where he lives." I was grabbing at my hair in hot handfuls, almost pulling it out.

I shouted, swore, bellowed at the tree that had my bike tied up in its high branches. But all my rage and frustration was aimed at Nottingham. I shouted so damn loud I reckoned he might have been able to hear me no matter which street he lived on.

"This is crazy," Mish said. "Totally crazy."

"Nottingham picked the right tree, then," Zoe said.

Nobody laughed.

"You know he's done it as revenge for what happened in *Spider Trap*, don't you?" Mish said to me.

I curled my lip. "Nottingham got a few cobwebs in his face and some spider bites," I scoffed. "Big deal."

"What you did was a mean and crappy trick," Mish told me. "You know it was. You started it."

"He put my bike up a tree," I shouted, jabbing my finger in the air.

Mish nodded. "Exactly. He's decided to go twice as mean, twice as crappy."

"Yeah, well," I said. "Watch me go three times, four times, five times."

Mish shook her head at me. I realised she did that more and more these days. I hated that she kept acting so big and clever, like she was so much smarter than me all the time.

Suddenly my anger was aimed at her. "If you're not even going to help me get my bike back, then why don't you just get lost?" I yelled at Mish. "Go home and do stupid French for school instead, if that's more important to you."

She stepped away from me, shocked. And I turned away so I didn't have to see the hurt in her eyes.

"You can't climb, so you can't help," I told Mish, despite having my back to her. Then I looked at Zoe and asked her. "You've climbed *Crazy Ash Bastard* before, haven't you? Can you help me get my bike down?"

I didn't watch Mish walk away across the moonlit football pitch. I stepped up to the tree.

CHAPTER 10

Climbing *Crazy Ash Bastard* was dangerous. Climbing in the dark was dangerous. That was why me and Zoe went slow and careful.

Harvey had finally made it back to the park. He stood with his brother watching us. The pair of them were soon nothing more than chunky black shadows far below.

Most ash trees weren't that difficult to climb. They had springy but strong branches that could take quite a bit of weight. They weren't too bushy with leaves so that you couldn't see where you were putting your feet or reaching with your hands. And you didn't get many bugs and insects living in them. If you asked me, I reckoned ash trees were maybe the most beautiful trees too. But not this one.

In the old days, before I was born, people in the village used to saw off and steal branches from this tree. I supposed because ash wood was

great for making furniture and stuff. A special
village law had to be passed to stop people doing
it in case they killed the tree altogether. But lots
of damage had already been done and whatever
bits of branches that had been left grew in
strange ways over the years. They seemed to
stick out at wrong angles or end in ugly stumps.
Like I said, ash trees should look beautiful. This
one looked crazy.

Zoe and I had to feel in the dark for the
good branches as we climbed. It was extra-slow
going. We helped each other as much as we could,
pointing out which foothold was safe, which was
too risky. If I hadn't been so mad and angry at
Nottingham, I reckoned I might have thought of
this as one of my most daring climbs.

"Sorry if I kind of forced you into helping," I
said to Zoe. "But you know Marvin and Harvey
can't climb like you. Especially not in the dark. It
proves you've got *reach*."

"You shouldn't have told Mish to go home," Zoe
said.

"She can't climb," I said. "She couldn't have
helped."

Zoe tested a branch. It held. She went higher. "Mish is meant to be your best friend," she said.

The branch I was holding didn't feel strong enough. "She doesn't act like it much these days," I said. "She's changing."

"You don't say," Zoe replied. "Maybe you'll start puberty too, one day."

"Shut up. You know what I mean." I yanked on a different branch, but it snapped off in my hand. "It's Friday night and Mish is doing homework."

Zoe showed me which branch was stronger. "I heard her talking to Miss Jaden after class last week. And she said Mish was one of the cleverest kids in our year."

"We all knew that anyway," I said as I waited for Zoe to move up one branch higher and then followed.

"But Miss Jaden said Mish should start using her brain properly if she really did want to go to university one day," Zoe went on.

"Why's Mish even thinking about university when we're only fifteen?" I asked. "That's crazy." I missed my footing in the dark and had to cling on tight. "I bet she changes her mind in a couple of years."

"I bet she doesn't," Zoe said. "But I bet you she'd be really happy if you said you wanted to go with her."

"Why would I want to go to university?" I used the same branch as Zoe, scrambling after her.

"Because university isn't this little, tiny, itty-bitty, boring, dead-end village in the middle of nowhere," Zoe said. "Mish told me she doesn't want to still be here when she's as old as her mum."

"I like it here," I said.

Did I feel guilty about telling Mish to go home? Maybe I would later. After we'd rescued my bike.

We made it to where Nottingham had tied my bike to the tree. We were about three quarters of the way up. He'd wrapped rope round and round my bike frame and looped even more rope around the trunk.

"I still don't get how the hell Nottingham got it up so damn high," I said to Zoe.

"He climbed up with the rope first and then pulled your bike up after him," she said.

"That's amazing," I said, and I realised I really meant it.

"You've got to admit," Zoe said. "He's got *reach*."

But I wasn't going to go that far.

Zoe shouted down to Marvin and Harvey, telling them that we were going to lower the bike to them. We squatted among the branches and began untying the rope one knot at a time.

"My mum got me this bike," I said. "I know she must have saved up for ages to buy it. Especially on her crappy wages. And if Nottingham's damaged it in any way, I swear I'll make him regret it. It's the best thing I've got."

Zoe grunted as she struggled with the rope and the massive knots Nottingham had tied. I couldn't see any scratches on the bike's paintwork, but it was too dark to look properly.

"I've got to get Nottingham back for this," I said to Zoe. "You agree with me that Mish is wrong to say I shouldn't get revenge on him, don't you?"

Zoe laughed. "What happened today has been the most interesting thing to happen around here in ages," she said, "with you and Nottingham getting in each other's faces. I can't wait for Sunday to see you two racing to climb the last tree."

"I'll win," I said. "I'm the best climber in the village."

"So you keep telling everyone."

"I'm going to call it *Sullivan's Skystabber*."

"We know," Zoe said.

"You think *King Big and Tall* is a crap name too, don't you?" I went on.

Zoe didn't answer but handed me the end of the rope. "When I untie this last knot," she said, "you better be holding tight. Maybe if you wrap the rope around the trunk it will be easier to lower your bike down."

"It's OK," I told Zoe. "My bike's not that heavy. It can't be heavy if Nottingham managed to drag it all the way up here, right?"

She nodded. "OK, careful, hold it," she said. "Last knot …"

But my bike was heavy enough to pull that final knot undone all by itself. I felt the rope jerk in my grip. I grabbed hold tight. The weight of the bike dragged me forward and I almost lost my footing.

"Keep hold!" Zoe shouted.

I grunted and pulled back hard. The rope burned the palms of my hands.

It took me a split second to realise that if I kept hold of the rope I was going to get yanked right off the branch, right out of the tree.

I let the rope go.

I watched my bike fall. It crashed down past the branches, slipping and sliding between the leaves in the darkness. It felt like my stomach fell with it.

Zoe shouted a warning. Marvin and Harry dived out of the way.

My bike smashed and shattered when it hit the ground.

PART 4
Double Trunker

Oak (*Quercus robur*)

Deciduous – Europe – 25 metres

CHAPTER 11

I carried my bike all the way home. It had hit the ground with its back wheel first and that wheel had been crushed with the impact. The spokes had exploded from the wheel's shattered rim. The whole frame was bent and twisted. The seat had popped off like a cork from a bottle of sparkling wine. My precious bike was a mess.

I walked away across the park and didn't dare say a word to Marvin, Harvey or Zoe. Marvin offered to help me carry my bike, but I just shook my head. I was worried that if I tried to speak, if I even opened my mouth, I'd start crying.

I struggled home with my wrecked bike and hid it right at the back of our overgrown garden, like a dirty secret. All the time I was trying to think up an explanation for Mum. How could I tell her what had happened? She had worked so hard and saved so much to buy me that bike. I didn't have a clue what to say.

It was almost midnight, but Mum still wasn't home from work. Nev was watching TV in the living room. I headed straight upstairs to my room and sprawled on my bed without taking off my clothes or even my Swift Runs. That was when I began to cry. I pulled the pillow over my head and sobbed.

My hatred for Nottingham burned like a bonfire inside me.

CHAPTER 12

Waking up the next morning was tough. I'd dreamed it had been me who'd fallen from *Crazy Ash Bastard*, not my bike. Maybe I wished that was exactly what had happened.

I reckoned I was more tired than I'd been the night before. I didn't want to get out of bed. So I stayed deep under the duvet listening to bits of conversation between Mum and Nev downstairs. No way did I want to join in.

At just after nine Mum knocked on my closed door and told me that she was going to the supermarket. She reminded me not to forget my homework. I heard Mum walk down the stairs, open the front door, close it behind her, start the car and drive away. But I still didn't get out of bed.

The house was quiet. I wondered if Nev had gone out too. All I did was stare at the ceiling, trying to decide if I should tell Mum my bike had been stolen. I decided to charge my phone for the first time in weeks, thinking I could call Mish and ask her what I should do. But I didn't even know if Mish was talking to me any more.

I wished I hadn't got angry with her last night. But I wished she wasn't changing so much. Suddenly my friendship with Mish felt as wrecked as my bike and that made me want to cry all over again.

What at last got me up and out of bed was knowing that I didn't want to face Mum when she came home again. She'd only need a second to suss something was wrong with me. Avoiding her seemed so much easier than lying to her.

I told myself I'd go to the park and have a practice climb on the last tree. If I didn't beat Nottingham to the top tomorrow and didn't get to name the tree, then everything – EVERYTHING – would be the worst ever!!!

I went to use the bathroom. Nev was just coming out and he'd stunk up the place to high heaven.

"So what was last night all about, then?" Nev asked. His face was pale and shiny, no doubt from a headache and hangover.

"Nothing," I said.

"Didn't seem like nothing," Nev said.

Maybe there are some younger brothers who can ask their big brothers for help and advice. Not in this house.

I decided to dodge the stench Nev had left in the bathroom. I grabbed my rubbish phone despite it being nowhere near fully charged and headed downstairs and outside.

Another hot day. I walked to the park but didn't go near any of the trees yet. There was no one in the play area, so I sat on a tiny swing and phoned Mish. She didn't answer. I tried to think of another time, ever, when I'd called Mish and she hadn't answered. How come yesterday I'd had friends and a cool bike, and I'd been the best climber in the village too, but today everything had gone so bad?

Nottingham.

All his fault.

CHAPTER 13

Spiteful ideas popped into my head as I dangled on the swing. I thought about smashing Nottingham's bedroom window by chucking massive branches through it. But I didn't know where he lived and I reckoned I'd end up in worse trouble doing something like that anyway. No, I decided the best revenge would be beating Nottingham to the top of the last tree. I would prove I had *reach* and was still the best climber in the village. It would feel sweet and glorious.

I crossed the park thinking I was going to practise climbing the tree that would soon be called *Sullivan's Skystabber*. But halfway across I decided I just wanted to get up high and see the view. Getting above everything down here normally made me feel better.

The best tree for a wide and amazing view was the oak we called *Double Trunker*. It was the second-tallest tree of the Big Five and sometime in the past it had been sliced almost completely in two by a huge lightning strike.

The lightning hadn't killed the tree. Over the years its two halves had carried on growing, together but always separate. There was a gap between its two trunks that got wider as they reached higher. Down low you could jump from trunk to trunk as you climbed. At the top the gap was so wide you'd need to be damn brave, or plain stupid, to try leaping across.

We often had races on *Double Trunker*. Despite its height it was the easiest of the Big Five to climb. Oak tree branches were always thick and sturdy, and *Double Trunker* didn't have too many leaves that could get in your face. Some said the south-side trunk was easier than the north-side, so we always flipped a coin to see who got which trunk to race up. The loser was normally pelted with handfuls of acorns. I didn't care. I'd never been pelted with acorns because I'd never even met a climber who could come close to beating me on either trunk.

For no real reason this morning I chose the south-side trunk. The sun was strong and by the time I made it to the top I was sweaty and wished I had a bottle of water. I'd been looking forward to the view. But it was totally spoiled by Nottingham, who was sitting on the north-side trunk.

CHAPTER 14

Nottingham and I looked like a pair of gargoyles as we faced each other on the tree's split trunk, clinging to the highest branches. I wanted to leap across and knock him off his perch, but the gap was too wide. There was nothing around us except clear blue sky, and the grass below seemed very far away.

Nottingham was wearing the same cap and clothes as yesterday, and I reckoned he looked much more like a gargoyle than me. The spider bites on his face and neck had swollen up all red and nasty. They looked painful. It was like he had rotten bubbles pushing up from under his skin. A couple were scratched bloody. I guessed he'd say the bites were my fault, but I refused to feel guilty.

"What're you doing up here?" I shouted across to him.

"Free tree, free park, free country," Nottingham said. "Just doing the same as you, I guess. Enjoying the view."

I thought that really he'd come here to practise for tomorrow's contest, like me.

"Your face is ruining my view," I said.

Nottingham touched one of the painfully bloated bites on his forehead and winced. He turned and pointed at *Crazy Ash Bastard*. "I see you got your bike down."

"My bike's wrecked," I said. "It fell."

He looked honestly shocked. "I didn't mean that to happen," he said. "It was meant to be a joke."

"No one's laughing," I said.

"I would've got your bike down for you again," Nottingham said. He touched his face again and added, "But after the *Spider Trap*, I just wanted to get my own back and piss you off."

"Well done, it worked," I said. "Yesterday I just thought you were a knob-head, but today I totally hate you."

"I just said I didn't mean for your bike to get wrecked, didn't I? But you started it."

"Started what? How?" I asked.

Nottingham pointed at his face. "With this?"

"I didn't start anything," I said. "Because of you I had to carry my bike home."

We glared at each other, our anger reflected in each other's faces.

"Why don't you climb down and get lost?" I said.

"Why don't you?" Nottingham replied.

We both sat down on opposite branches, our legs dangling. Neither of us was going to climb down just yet.

"The only reason you don't want me around is because you know I'm a good climber," Nottingham said. "That's true, isn't it? You feel threatened."

"You've not got *reach*," I said.

"Don't you think *reach* is about more than just how high you can climb?" Nottingham asked.

I ignored his question and asked one of my own. "Why did you even come here? Everything was good until you turned up and started climbing our trees."

"Whose trees? They're not anybody's. And believe me, I didn't choose to come here. All I wanted to do yesterday was join in with what you do around here. I was trying to make friends. How was I to know that climbing your trees is something precious that only true-blood villagers are allowed to do?"

"You were showing off," I said. "You reckon that you're a better climber than me."

Nottingham looked away into the distance, but I heard him say, "Maybe I am a better climber than you."

I swayed on the branch I was sitting on, leaning forward as much as I dared. I wished again I could reach him, grab him, punch him.

Nottingham turned to glare at me across the gap. "You were showing off just as bad," he said. "Worse. Getting all up in my face and saying you'd get my cap back."

"I was trying to help."

"Bollocks. You were showing off too. *I'm the best climber in the village,*" Nottingham mimicked me.

I ripped a handful of acorns off the closest branch.

"You know, I've been asking a couple of the other kids about you," Nottingham said. "There's some people around here who think you're a right arsehole."

I shook my head. "As if."

But then I thought about when Nottingham asked the other climbers yesterday, "Who wants to see me beat Sully to the top of this tree?" I remembered feeling surprised by how many of my so-called friends had put their hands in the air. I thought about how Marvin or Harvey or Zoe could have easily stopped him from hauling my bike up *Crazy Ash Bastard*. Hadn't Marvin said he'd thought it was funny?

I glared across at Nottingham, wanting to say he was talking rubbish, but I kept my mouth shut. I squeezed the acorns tight in my fist.

Nottingham sneered at me and said, "Don't you think the others get sick and tired of you going on about how you're the 'best climber in the village'? Over and over again. Blah, blah, blah."

"They're just jealous," I said.

"Blah, blah, blah," Nottingham repeated.

I felt hurt and anxious. I didn't know what else to do, so I chucked my handful of acorns at him. "You're the arsehole."

Nottingham ducked and wobbled on his branch. But to be honest, me throwing them was pointless and pathetic. One bounced harmlessly off his chest and the rest flew wide.

He grabbed a handful of his own acorns from the nearest branch and threw them at me. One hit my cheek, another clonked off my thick skull, but they didn't hurt.

We spent five minutes chucking tiny acorns at each other. I chucked, he chucked. They were the worst weapons in the world. No one was ever going to win. It was weirdly funny. I realised we were both smiling and I stopped throwing them.

"Why don't you piss off back to Sherwood Forest or wherever?" I said, trying to sound at least a bit tough.

"I wish I could," Nottingham said, looking miserable.

"So why don't you?" I pushed.

He hesitated a long time before saying anything. I reckoned he was deciding whether to tell me the truth or not.

"Because I've got nowhere else to go," Nottingham admitted. "I got dumped here, at my cousin's house, and I don't even know where *here* is."

"So why come in the first place?" I asked.

"I keep telling you," he said. "I didn't have a choice." And I thought he was going to scratch at the spider bites on his face but instead he touched his scar. I didn't think he even knew he was doing it.

"Did you get that falling out of a tree?" I asked. "A Sherwood Forest tree?"

Nottingham jerked his fingers away from his face and the look in his eyes made me wish I hadn't asked. He didn't look angry. He was scared, or maybe sad. Both at once.

"My dad did it," Nottingham said. "I got him mad. I was always making him mad even if I didn't mean to. And so now I'm stuck here, wherever *here* is, so he can't find me."

We both swayed a bit on our tall branches. I didn't know what to say. I didn't know if he wanted me to say anything. A silence stretched across the gap between us. There was no strong breeze up here, but I felt cold anyway. I looked down. It was a long, long way to fall.

I looked back across at Nottingham and he met my stare with a challenge in his eye. I didn't know if it was a challenge to laugh at him or attack him or run off and spread his secrets around the whole village. I wasn't sure why he'd even wanted to tell me anything so honest and personal.

At last I said, "I don't know where my dad is. He left years ago. When I was a kid, I used to write to him without my mum knowing. I wrote him so many letters I had to steal stamps from the Post Office so she wouldn't find out. He's never written back. Not once."

Now it was Nottingham's turn to look awkward. We mirrored each other on our branches of *Double Trunker*.

"I won't tell anyone about your dad," I promised.

"I won't tell anyone about yours either," Nottingham said.

I laughed but didn't smile. "Don't worry, everyone around here knows about my messed-up family. But it's only Mish who knows about all the letters I wrote. She used to help me steal stamps."

"She seems cool," Nottingham said. "How long's she been your girlfriend?"

"She's not my girlfriend," I said. "But we're best friends." There was a stab of sharp splinters inside me as I said it. I hoped Mish was still my best friend. "She's totally brilliant and very cool." I shrugged. "But she's not my type. Not really. Why? Do you fancy her?"

Nottingham shrugged too. "Not really my type either."

I shuffled on my branch. He fidgeted on his.

"Listen," Nottingham said. "I swear, I honestly didn't mean for your bike to get smashed up."

"I totally wanted you to get a faceful of spiders," I said. "But maybe I didn't think it would be so damn bad."

"I itch like hell," he said.

I gazed out over *Double Trunker*'s canopy across the park, towards the streets and houses of the village. Then I shifted myself around on the high branch so I could look away from the village, over the roads and fields into the distance.

"How far is it to Sherwood Forest?" I asked. Maybe I was thinking about Zoe saying Mish wanted to go to university one day. Maybe I was trying to come up with somewhere I might want to go one day too.

"Four or five hours by car," Nottingham said. "Hopefully far enough for me, if you know what I mean."

I nodded, knowing he meant far enough away from his dad. And I realised I couldn't ever imagine leaving the village. At least not for good.

"You seriously don't reckon you could be the best climber in Sherwood Forest as well, do you?" Nottingham asked.

"With you as my only competition, it'll be a doddle," I said.

"If you say so."

I shuffled around on my branch again. Now I could see the last of the Big Five trees, looking so tall it might poke holes in a passing cloud. I pointed at it.

"*Sullivan's Skystabber*," I said.

"*King Big and Tall*," Nottingham replied.

"Guess we'll find out tomorrow," I said.

"Guess we will," he agreed.

I climbed down, leaving him up there.

PART 5
The Last Tree

Yew (*Taxus baccata*)

Evergreen – Europe, North Africa, Asia – 30 metres

CHAPTER 15

By Sunday morning, word about our competition had spread. The crowd around the last tree was twice as big as the one we'd had at *Spider Trap* on Friday. Faces all turned to watch me as I walked across the park towards them. I could feel the excited tension in the air. Most of the time I would have loved such a large audience. This morning it made me nervous. I felt like I had a lot to prove.

There was one face in the crowd I wanted to see more than any other. Mish. I didn't know if she'd be here after what had happened at *Crazy Ash Bastard*. I was happy and relieved when I spotted her standing to one side with Zoe, Marvin and Harvey. Zoe and Marvin were holding hands and Harvey was fiddling with his phone.

I moved past the crowd towards Mish, and a couple of kids patted me on the back or wished me good luck.

One of them shouted, "Sully for the top!" I waved and grinned.

Then someone else shouted, "It's the second-best climber in the village!" I ignored that as best as I could. But I remembered Nottingham telling me what some people had said about me behind my back. I didn't feel any happier if they were now going to say it to my face.

"I wasn't sure if you'd be here," I said to Mish.

"I'm always here," she said. "Where else would I be?"

"Doing homework?"

"What's wrong with me doing homework all of a sudden?" Mish asked.

"Because it's all of a sudden," I said. "You've never been bothered before. Zoe said you're going to go to university."

"Maybe. I hope so. But not until I'm eighteen."

"So it's true? You really do want to?" I asked.

"So what if I want to? Miss Jaden said I could go if I did well enough this year and stayed at school to do my A levels."

Why did the thought of Mish leaving the village and going to university scare me so much? It was worse than even the most difficult climb, even the most painful fall. "But you said it yourself, you're crap at school," I said.

Mish looked hurt, like I'd punched her in the guts. "Miss Jaden doesn't think so. She says I've just got to catch up with the lessons I missed when I was looking after my mum. And Harvey's helping me. We finished all the French stuff yesterday and I'm beginning to get it now."

I glared at Harvey, but he didn't notice because he was staring at his phone like always.

"What about us? The best climber in the village needs a support crew," I half-joked.

Mish didn't find it even half-funny. "It gets kind of boring just being support crew all the time. And I've realised that's all I'll ever be for you, right? So why stay here? I want to do something special with my life."

"So do I," I said, jabbing a finger at the tree right in front of us. "I'm going to beat Nottingham to the top – show everyone I'm still the best climber and name the last tree. I'm going to prove just how much *reach* I've got."

Mish sighed. "Great, for *you*. And I'll always be known as just some girl who hung around with the climber who named the last tree."

"But don't you want me to name the tree?" I asked.

"Of course I do," Mish said. "Obviously. But that's not the whole point, is it?"

It was for me.

Harvey finally looked up from his phone. "Don't you think having *reach* should mean more than just how high you can climb?" he asked.

"*Ferme ta bouche*," I told him.

CHAPTER 16

It was ten o'clock and still no Nottingham. A few people began to whisper that maybe he'd chickened out. I didn't think he'd dare to chicken out. But the crowd was getting restless and I wondered what on earth he was up to. All this hanging around was just making me more nervous. And I wondered if that was Nottingham's plan. He wanted me worked up, stressed out, anxious, nervous. Then I'd make more mistakes climbing.

So I told myself to relax.

I'd been up early preparing. I'd used a knife from the kitchen on the soles of my Swift Runs, cutting slashes to deepen the treads. I'd taken a pair of Mum's leather gloves and rubbed sandpaper on the palms and fingertips to make them extra rough and grippy. Not only was I wearing my favourite baseball cap but I also had an old pair of swimming goggles for added eye protection. Under my jogging bottoms I was wearing skateboard pads on my knees. Finally, I had a water bottle on a strap across my chest. But I'd filled it with Red Bull, not water.

I was ready for the climb of my life.

"If Nottingham's not here by ten past," I told the crowd, "I'll climb without him."

He arrived at nine minutes past. And he was riding a bike. *My* bike.

Nottingham came through the park gates pedalling hard and sped across the footy pitch towards us. The crowd around the last tree parted for him when they realised he wasn't going to slow down. He pulled a big roundhouse skid in the grass to stop in front of me.

"What?" I asked. "What the hell ...?"

His face was still messed up and blotchy with bites, but he was grinning like the Pope had promised to make him a saint or something. "I fixed your bike," he said.

"Is this some kind of trick?" I asked.

"I felt bad," Nottingham told me. "Like I said yesterday, the last thing I meant to happen was for your bike to get smashed up. So I sneaked into your back garden and stole it. Again. I used bits from my cousin's bike. He'll never notice because he never uses it. I replaced the back wheel, the seat and managed to get your frame as straight as possible too. It took me all night. But ..." Nottingham waved his arm as if he was the world's greatest magician. "I fixed your bike."

Marvin came over to have a look. "That's so cool," he said. "You really did this by yourself? It looks almost new."

I glanced across at Mish and all she could do was shrug. I turned back to Nottingham. "Why?" I said. "I don't get it ..."

His big wide grin slipped a bit. "I just told you why," Nottingham said. "I felt bad." He wheeled the bike towards me, trying to make me take it from him.

But no way was I going to touch it.

"This doesn't change anything," I said. I poked a finger in his chest. "If you're trying to get out of climbing ... You were the one who wrecked my bike in the first place."

"To be fair," Marvin said. "You and Zoe wrecked it."

Zoe punched him in the arm.

"I'm not trying to get out of anything," Nottingham said. "I thought I was doing you a favour."

Harvey took the bike to one side and looked it over. "Now this is *reach*," he declared, impressed.

But it was a hundred per cent not the way I'd expected things to be. Even after what Nottingham and I had told each other at the top of *Double Trunker* yesterday we were still enemies, weren't we? He was still an outsider. And I was protecting our tree from being named by him.

"Nothing's changed," I said. "I'm still going to beat you to the top of the tree."

Nottingham pulled his baseball cap down low, hiding his eyes in the shadow of the cap's peak.

"If you say so," he replied.

CHAPTER 17

Zoe held her closed fists out towards Nottingham and me. "Which hand?" she said to Nottingham.

He tapped the back of Zoe's left fist with his finger. But when she opened her fist, it was empty. Zoe opened her right fist to show the leaf she was clutching and said, "Sully's first up. As soon as he falls, *if* he falls, Nottingham can try."

The crowd moved back to give me room but still nudged each other for the best view. I put my swimming goggles on, then my baseball cap, then my gloves. My whole body was buzzing. I told myself to stay calm and to focus. There were a few shouts and calls from the crowd, cheering me on. I stepped up to the huge trunk of the last tree. I knew that it took at least three people with arms stretched wide to be able to touch fingertips around the tree. That was how big it was.

It was a yew tree, scarred and gnarled and hundreds of years old. The bark was a reddish-brown and the trunk had massive grooves running vertically down it, looking as if it was made up of columns, or maybe even a dozen trunks all squashed together. And there was a lot of trunk before you could even reach the branches. The lowest branch was still higher than my head.

I looked for deep grooves in the bark where I might be able to get a good grip and wondered if Nottingham had brought gloves too. Everything about yew trees was poisonous to humans. Their soft needles, red berries and even the bark. I guessed there was more than one reason this formidable tree had never been climbed. Yews were also known as trees of the dead, after all.

I spotted a lumpy knot on the trunk about knee-height. I reckoned if I could get my foot on that I might be able to jump up and launch myself to grab a branch.

The crowd had been moving with me, following me around the trunk, everyone wanting to see. They were silent as I got my foot onto the lumpy knot and stood up straight, my arms wide, hugging the tree's trunk. I was off the ground. If I put a foot back down, it would be classed as a "fall" and Nottingham would get the chance to climb.

I was sure the climb would be simpler once I was up among the branches. I could feel the rough bark against my cheek and smell the wood. My chest and belly were flat to the trunk as I hugged it to my body. I tilted my head back to look above me. I could jump and try to grab for the first branch, but I didn't think I'd make it. So I lifted my left foot, feeling with the toe of my Swift Run for a crack or crevice. No luck. I shifted my balance, tried with my right foot and found a rut in the bark that I could wedge my toe inside.

I managed to stand up straight again from the rut, locking my knee. When I looked up, that first low branch was closer. Still hugging the massive trunk, I inched my hands higher. But I felt my toe slipping from the rut. I had to jump. My fingertips brushed the branch but missed and I fell to the ground.

I landed and rolled.

The crowd "oohed".

Nottingham stepped forward. I reluctantly moved aside to let him get close to the tree. He walked around the trunk the same as I had – looking for something like a secret "key" in the bark that would unlock the way up.

Nottingham shooed the crowd further back. I saw he was going to use the same lumpy knot I'd tried but in a different way. He took big backward steps away from the tree. Then with a run-up he jumped, slapped the sole of his trainer against the knot and leapt high, arms reaching, hands clutching, fingers grabbing. And just like that he was hanging from the first branch. It bent under his weight, but there was no crack or snap.

The gathered kids gasped. A couple of them started clapping and cheering. I watched nervously as Nottingham moved hand-over-hand along the branch until he could plant both feet flat on the trunk. He walked up it, swung a leg over and climbed astride the branch, making it seem easy.

He looked down at me. *"King Big and Tall,"* he whispered.

He managed to get his feet under him to crouch on the branch. He tilted his head back, looking up through the leaves and speckled patches of sunshine. There was a big grin smeared across his face. My belly was filled with a jittery panic. I thought he was going to make it higher. But he made a mistake as he went to

reach above him. The sole of his trainer slipped.
And gravity hates an over-confident climber.

Nottingham fell further and harder than I
had. He cried out as he hit the ground. I hoped
he hadn't broken anything. I wanted to beat him,
not for him to be forced to back out because of
injury.

I stepped over him as he lay there clutching
his arm. My turn again.

CHAPTER 18

Almost an hour later, both of us were filthy, sore and tired. The day was getting hotter. The crowd was beginning to get bored. Even Harvey had stopped taking photos. Nottingham and I had four then five, six then seven tries each at the climb, and neither of us could properly get off the ground and into the tree.

Fall after fall. My shoulder throbbed from bashing it on the ground so much. Nottingham's scar was bright pink with sweaty exhaustion.

Then Mish shouted, "Why don't you do it together? Help each other?"

I shot her a look like she was a traitor.

"It's the only way you'll ever climb it," Mish said to me. "What's more important? Saying you've climbed it together, or never climbing it at all?"

Many of the kids in the crowd agreed with her. A chant of "Together, together, together" began, growing louder.

I hated the idea.

Nottingham was nodding. "She's right," he said to me. "This is crazy. We aren't good enough climbers to do it by ourselves."

I hated him saying that even more.

"Look," Nottingham said. "I'll boost you up to grab one of the lower branches, then you can pull me up after you. We could definitely make it to the top together."

I wanted to ask, *Then who'll be the one who gets to name the tree?* But I kept my mouth shut and simply nodded. The crowd cheered, happy there was going to be something interesting happening again. I looked at Mish and she smiled at me. When I didn't smile back, her smile slipped and she shook her head. She knew me so well. And she'd guessed what I was going to do next.

"Don't," she mouthed silently.

I ignored her. Mish wanted to go to university. She wanted to leave me behind. Why should I take any notice of her?

Nottingham leaned his back against the trunk and laced the fingers of both his hands together to make a step.

"Ready?" I asked.

"Ready," he agreed.

I ran at Nottingham, sprang forward and planted my foot into his hands. He grunted as he lifted me up with all his strength, almost throwing me into the tree. I flew. I grabbed the lowest thick branch in both hands and swung myself up onto it.

I got the biggest cheer of the morning from the crowd. But when I looked down, the only two people I saw were Mish and Nottingham. He had his hand raised, waiting for me to pull him up after me. Mish was still shaking her head, far from happy, because she'd guessed what I was going to do next.

I turned away from both Mish and Nottingham, faced the branches above me and started climbing higher.

CHAPTER 19

I didn't see how Nottingham finally managed to get up into the tree. Maybe it was Marvin or another climber from the crowd who helped him. Or maybe it was his rage at me cheating him that gave him the extra boost he needed. But now the race was on.

I looked down between fringes of needle-like leaves, but all I could see was the top of Nottingham's black baseball cap. He was chasing me.

I wasn't thinking about the crowd or Mish or my bike or anything. All I cared about was getting higher and being the first to the top. *Sullivan's Skystabber.* Branch after branch after branch. Solid grip, steady feet. Keep close to the trunk. Balance. Breathe. Next branch. Higher. Pull myself up. Climb higher.

Nottingham sounded like a roaring bull below me, huffing and puffing. He was crashing up past the branches, and the tree shook and shuddered around me as he came.

I tried to focus on my own fast but steady climbing. I was over halfway up. But the thought of Nottingham underneath me made me careless. I tried to use branches that were too thin and snapped easily. Twice, three times my Swift Runs slipped, and my heart was louder than a heavy-metal drummer as I grabbed the trunk for balance. But I couldn't slow down. Next branch, next branch. Higher. And Nottingham was even closer.

He wasn't a bull, I realised. He was more like a missile aimed at me. Blasting towards me. I wondered how worried I should be about him exploding. And he was getting closer.

When I dared to look again, Nottingham was so close he could have yanked on my ankle and pulled me down. His swollen face was slick with sweat, red with anger. His scar throbbed. He stared up at me. He hated me. I could see it blazing in his eyes.

This realisation shocked me. Had anyone truly hated me before? Had I ever given anyone this much reason to hate me before? Did I deserve Nottingham's hate?

I stopped climbing like I'd hit an invisible ceiling.

I didn't want Nottingham to hate me. I didn't want anyone to hate me. I wanted people to think I had *reach*. I wanted them to be impressed by how good at climbing I was. But more than anything, I wanted them to like me. Yet Nottingham glared at me with rotten hate filling up his eyes.

After talking together at the top of *Double Trunker* yesterday, and after him mending my bike, I suddenly realised how much I *liked* him.

I crouched as low as I could on the branch I was standing on. I went to reach down to him, to take his hand in mine and pull him up.

Nottingham must have thought I was going to hit him.

He flinched away from me. He let go of the branch he was holding.

He slipped.

He fell.

CHAPTER 20

All I could do was watch from my branch near the top. I felt the shudders of the tree all around me. Nottingham fell fast. He smashed against the branches, tumbling and tumbling as he fell. And maybe I imagined the biggest shudder of all when he hit the ground.

The crowd down there surged around Nottingham, blocking him from view. Their terrified, babbling voices rose up to me. The excitement of the day had vanished. Everyone was scared.

I started climbing back down.

My belly was full of rolling snowballs, churning round and round. Every beat of my heart was like a hammer smashing against ice. The cold inside me was so intense that I wanted to puke. I felt like I was climbing down from the tree into a slippery endless black hole. I could only go slowly because every few seconds I needed to wipe frightened tears from my eyes to be able to see.

The ambulance had already arrived by the time I made it to the ground.

"What happened?" Mish wanted to know.

I sat down. Now that I'd stopped climbing, my legs had turned to melting jelly. "It was an accident," I said. "Nottingham slipped. I tried to ... But he slipped."

Mish put her arm around me and hugged me, even if I didn't deserve it.

We all watched as Nottingham was carried on a stretcher into the ambulance by the paramedics. I wanted to ask if he was still alive. Instead I puked my guts up on the roots of the last of the Big Five.

PART 6
The Reach

Our Tree (*arbor nostri*)

Forever – Right Here – Massive

CHAPTER 21

Afterwards, the village council put up short metal fences around the trees to stop us from climbing them. It worked ... for a few weeks. Plenty of kids started climbing again that summer. But not me.

Nottingham was messed up bad. He'd broken this, that and everything. The doctors said it would take a lot of hard work and time before he could even walk again.

Going to visit him in hospital felt like the hardest thing I'd ever had to do. Climbing the hospital stairs took ten times more bravery than climbing any of the Big Five. The room they kept him in felt too bright and too unfriendly. I saw Nottingham lying there in the stiff-sheeted bed, with beeping monitors and everything in plaster and tubes coming out his nose, and I wanted to puke all over again. I just stood in the doorway and we stared at each other for what seemed like hours before either of us spoke.

I said, "At least your spider bites have got better."

Nottingham didn't laugh, he cried. And I cried too.

"I'm sorry," I said.

"It wasn't just you," he said.

"If you say so."

"Who are the best climbers?" Nottingham asked me.

"The ones who bounce back," I replied.

I started going to see him most days. At first it was guilt making me go, I suppose. But it didn't take long for me to look forward to visiting Nottingham. The nurses started saying hello to me because I was there so often.

We talked a lot about trees and we boasted a lot about climbing. Nottingham still liked talking about climbing and some of his stories about the Sherwood Forest trees sounded amazing. But neither of us knew if he'd ever be able to climb again. So I changed the subject a lot and we talked about movies, music and sometimes even school too.

Mish came with me to visit him sometimes. The first time she came, Nottingham looked honestly surprised when we walked into his hospital room together.

"Are you two friends again then?" he asked.

Mish laughed. "Again?" she said. "When did he stop being my friend?" She pointed at me. "Sully's *my* support crew now."

"She's the cleverest brainbox in the village," I said.

At last Nottingham was allowed to leave hospital, and I still went to see him at his cousin's house. It would have felt strange not to. His cousin loved bikes more than trees, but he was cool and didn't mind me hanging around all the time. I helped Nottingham do his exercises to make his legs and his back stronger.

One day Nottingham asked me, "Are you just trying to fix me like I fixed your bike?"

"I wish your cousin had more spare parts," I answered.

I was beginning to believe that maybe our friendship had *reach*. And I reckoned that if

Nottingham ever told me his real name, it would mean he'd forgiven me.

CHAPTER 22

Late one night that summer, Mish and I sneaked into the park through the gap in the hedges we knew about. I had a short plank of wood that I'd sanded and painted and made into a sign. Mish helped me get over the new fence around the last of the Big Five and passed me the hammer and nails. I fixed the sign to the yew tree's trunk.

It read: "The Reach".

We named it, even though no one ever made it to the top.

*With thanks to the Vienna Quarantine
Writers, Uni-Verse, Paul Malone
and SWC. As well as Lucy Juckes,
Ailsa Bathgate and the Barrington Stoke
team. All my love to Jasmine.*

Our books are tested
for children and young people by
children and young people.

Thanks to everyone who consulted on
a manuscript for their time and effort in
helping us to make our books better
for our readers.

KU-306-127

READ MORE FLAT STANLEY ADVENTURES
by
JEFF BROWN

FLAT
STANLEY

STANLEY AND THE
MAGIC LAMP

INVISIBLE
STANLEY

STANLEY
IN SPACE

STANLEY'S CHRISTMAS
ADVENTURE

STANLEY,
FLAT AGAIN!

FLAT STANLEY

STANLEY

INVISIBLE
STANLEY

JEFF BROWN

Illustrated by Rob Biddulph

Farshore

For Max and Louis

Farshore

First published in Great Britain 1985
by Methuen Children's Books Ltd

Reissued 2017 by Farshore

An imprint of HarperCollins*Publishers*
1 London Bridge Street, London SE1 9GF

farshore.co.uk

HarperCollins*Publishers*
1st Floor, Watermarque Building,
Ringsend Road, Dublin 4, Ireland

Text copyright © 1985 Jeff Brown
Illustrations copyright © 2017 Rob Biddulph

ISBN 978 1 4052 8805 7
Printed in Great Britain by CPI Group
4

A CIP catalogue record for this title is available from the British Library

All rights reserved. No part of this publication may be reproduced,
stored in a retrieval system, or transmitted, in any form or by any means,
electronic, mechanical, photocopying, recording or otherwise, without
the prior permission of the publisher and copyright owner.

Stay safe online. Any website addresses listed in this book are correct at the
time of going to print. However, Farshore is not responsible for content
hosted by third parties. Please be aware that online content can be subject
to change and websites can contain content that is unsuitable for children.
We advise that all children are supervised when using the internet.

MIX
Paper from
responsible sources
FSC™ C007454

This book is produced from independently certified FSC™ paper
to ensure responsible forest management.

For more information visit: www.harpercollins.co.uk/green

CONTENTS

MEET THE
LAMBCHOP
FAMILY

STANLEY

ARTHUR

MRS LAMBCHOP   **MR LAMBCHOP**

Once there was an ordinary kid called

Stanley Lambchop. A bulletin board

squashed him flat as a pancake.

Flat Stanley became famous – he even

foiled the art robbery of the century!

Stanley's little brother Arthur managed

to reinflate Stanley with a bicycle

pump, but ever since weird stuff just

keeps happening to Stanley . . .

Stanley Lambchop spoke into the darkness above his bed. 'I can't sleep. It's the rain, I think.'

There was no response from the bed across the room.

'I'm hungry too,' Stanley said. 'Are you awake, Arthur?'

'I am now,' said his younger brother. 'You woke me.'

Stanley fetched an apple from the

kitchen, and ate it by the bedroom
window. The rain had worsened.

'I'm still hungry,' he said.

'Raisins . . . shelf . . .' murmured Arthur,
half asleep again.

Crash! came thunder. Lightning flashed.

Stanley found the little box of raisins on a shelf by the window. He ate one.

Crash! Flash!

Stanley ate more raisins.

Crash! Flash!

Arthur yawned. 'Go to bed. You can't be hungry still.'

'I'm not, actually.' Stanley got back into bed. 'But I feel sort of . . . Oh, *different*, I guess.'

He slept.

CHAPTER 1
WHERE IS STANLEY?

'Breakfast is ready, George. We must wake the boys,' Mrs Lambchop said to her husband.

Just then Arthur Lambchop called from the bedroom he shared with his brother.

'Hey! Come here! Hey!'

Mr and Mrs Lambchop smiled, recalling another morning that had begun like this. An enormous bulletin board, they had discovered, had fallen on Stanley during

4

the night, leaving him unhurt but no more than half an inch thick. And so he had remained until Arthur blew him round again, weeks later, with a bicycle pump.

'Hey!' a call came again. 'Are you coming? Hey!'

Mrs Lambchop held firm views about good manners and correct speech. 'Hay is for horses, not people, Arthur,' she said as they entered the bedroom. 'As well you know.'

'Excuse me,' said Arthur. 'The thing is, I can *hear* Stanley, but I can't *find* him!'

Mr and Mrs Lambchop looked about the room. A shape was visible beneath the covers of Stanley's bed, and the pillow was squashed down, as if a head rested upon it. But there was no head.

'Why are you staring?' The voice was Stanley's.

Smiling, Mr Lambchop looked under the bed, but saw only a pair of slippers

and an old tennis ball. 'Not here,' he said.

Arthur put out a hand, exploring. 'Ouch!' said Stanley's voice. 'You poked my nose!' Arthur gasped.

Mrs Lambchop stepped forward. 'If I may . . .?' Gently, using both hands, she felt about.

A giggle rose from the bed. 'That *tickles*!'

'Oh, my!' said Mrs Lambchop.

She looked at Mr Lambchop and he at her, as they had during past great surprises. Stanley's flatness had been the first of these. Another had come the evening they discovered a young genie, Prince Haraz, in the bedroom with Stanley and Arthur, who had summoned him accidentally from a lamp.

Mrs Lambchop drew a deep breath. 'We must face facts, George. Stanley is now invisible.'

'You're *right*!' said a startled voice from the bed. 'I can't see my feet! Or my pyjamas!'

'Darndest thing I've ever seen,' said Mr Lambchop. 'Or *not* seen, I should say. Try some other pyjamas, Stanley.'

Stanley got out of bed, and put on different pyjamas, but these too vanished, reappearing when he took them off. It was the same with the shirt and slacks he tried next.

'Gracious!' Mrs Lambchop shook her head. 'How are we to keep track of you, dear?'

'I know!' said Arthur. Untying a small red balloon, a party favour, that floated above his bed, he gave Stanley the string to hold. 'Try this,' he said.

The string vanished, but not the balloon.

'There!' said Mrs Lambchop. 'At least we can tell, approximately, where Stanley is. Now let's all have breakfast. Then, George, we must see what Doctor Dan makes of this.'

CHAPTER 2
DOCTOR DAN

'What's that red balloon doing here?'
said Doctor Dan. 'Well, never mind.
Good morning, Mr and Mrs Lambchop.
Something about Stanley, my nurse says.
He's not been taken flat again?'

'No, no,' said Mrs Lambchop. 'Stanley
has remained round.'

'They mostly do,' said Doctor Dan.
'Well, let's have the little fellow in.'

'I am in,' said Stanley, standing directly

before him. 'Holding the balloon.'

'Ha, ha, Mr Lambchop!' said Doctor
Dan. 'You are an excellent ventriloquist!

But I see through your little joke!'
'What you see through,' said Mr
Lambchop, 'is Stanley.'

'Beg pardon?' said Doctor Dan.

'Stanley became invisible during the night,' Mrs Lambchop explained. 'We are quite unsettled by it.'

'Head ache?' Doctor Dan asked Stanley's balloon. 'Throat sore? Stomach upset?'

'I feel fine,' Stanley said.

'I see. Hmmmm . . .' Doctor Dan shook his head. 'Frankly, despite my long years of practice, I've not run into this before. But one of my excellent medical books, *Difficult and Peculiar Cases*, by Doctor Franz Gemeister, may help.'

He took a large book from the shelf behind him and looked into it.

'Ah! "Disappearances", page 134.' He found the page. 'Hmmmm . . . Not much here, I'm afraid. France, 1851: a Madame

Poulenc vanished while eating bananas in the rain. Spain, 1923: the Gonzales twins, aged 11, became invisible after eating fruit salad. Lightning had been observed. The most recent case, 1968, is Oombok, an Eskimo chief, last seen eating canned peaches during a blizzard.'

Doctor Dan returned the book to the shelf. 'That's all,' he said. 'Gemeister suspects a connection between bad weather and fruit.'

'It stormed last night,' said Stanley. 'And I ate an apple. Raisins, too.'

'There you are,' said Doctor Dan. 'But we must look at the bright side, Mr and Mrs Lambchop. Stanley seems perfectly healthy, except for the visibility factor. We'll just keep an eye on him.'

'Easier said than done,' said Mr

Lambchop. 'Why do his *clothes* also disappear?'

'Not my field, I'm afraid,' said Doctor Dan. 'I suggest a textile specialist.'

'We've kept you long enough, Doctor,' Mrs Lambchop said. 'Come, George, Stanley – Where *are* you, Stanley? Ah! Just hold the balloon a bit higher, dear.

Goodbye, Doctor Dan.'

By dinner time, Mr and Mrs Lambchop
and Arthur had become quite sad. The red
balloon, though useful in locating Stanley,
kept reminding them of how much they
missed his dear face and smile.

But after dinner, Mrs Lambchop, who
was artistically talented, replaced the
red balloon with a pretty white one
and got out her
watercolour paints
Using four colours
and several delicate
brushes, she painted
an excellent likeness
of Stanley, smiling,
on the white balloon.

WAITING ROOM

Everyone became at once more cheerful.
Stanley said he felt almost his old self
again, especially when he looked in the
mirror.

CHAPTER 3
THE FIRST DAYS

The next morning Mrs Lambchop wrote a note to Stanley's teacher, tied a stronger string to his balloon, and sent him off to school.

Dear Miss Benchley, the note said. *Stanley has unexpectedly become invisible. You will find the balloon a useful guide to his presence. Sincerely, Harriet Lambchop*

* * *

Miss Benchley spoke to the class. 'We must not stare at where we suppose Stanley to be,' she said. 'And not gossip about his state.'

Nevertheless, word soon reached a newspaper. A reporter visited the school and wrote a story for his paper.

The headline read: 'Smiling Student: Once You Saw Him, Now You Don't!' Beneath it were two photographs, a *Before* and an *After*.

The *Before*, taken by Miss Benchley a week earlier, showed a smiling Stanley at his desk. For the *After*, taken by the reporter, Stanley had posed the same way, but only the desk and his smiley-face balloon, bobbing above it, could be seen. The story included a statement by Miss Benchley that Stanley was in fact at the desk and, to the best of her knowledge, smiling.

Mr and Mrs Lambchop bought several copies of the paper for out-of-town friends. Her colourful balloon artwork lost something in black and white, Mrs Lambchop said, but on the whole it had photographed well.

Arthur said that *Invisible Boy's Brother* would have been an interesting picture, and that Stanley should suggest it if the reporter came round again.

Being invisible offered temptations, Mr and Mrs Lambchop said, but Stanley must resist them. It would be wrong to spy on people, for example, or sneak up to hear what they were saying.

But the next Saturday afternoon, when the Lambchops went to the movies, it was Arthur who could not resist.

'Don't buy a seat for Stanley,' he whispered at the ticket window. 'Just hide his balloon. Who'd know?'

'That would be deceitful, dear,' said Mrs Lambchop. 'Four seats, please,' she told the ticket lady. 'We want one for our coats, you see.'

'Wasn't *that* deceitful, sort of?' Arthur asked, as they went in.

'Not the same way,' said Mr Lambchop, tucking Stanley's balloon beneath his seat. Just as the film began, a very tall man sat directly in front of Stanley, blocking his view. Mr Lambchop took

Stanley on his lap, from which the screen was easily seen, and the people farther back saw right through him without knowing it. Stanley greatly enjoyed the show.

'See?' said Arthur, as they went out. 'Stanley didn't even *need* a seat.'

'You have a point,' said Mr Lambchop, whose legs had gone to sleep.

CHAPTER 4
IN THE PARK

It was Sunday afternoon. Arthur had gone to visit a friend, so Mr and Mrs Lambchop set out with Stanley for a nearby park. The streets were crowded, and Stanley carried his balloon, to lessen the risk of being jostled by people hurrying by.

Near the park, they met Ralph Jones, an old college friend of Mr Lambchop's.

'Always a treat running into your family,

George!' said Mr Jones. 'The older boy was flat once, I recall. You had him rolled up. And once you had a foreign student with you. A prince, yes?'

'What a memory you have!' said Mr Lambchop, remembering that he had introduced as a 'foreign student' the young genie with them at the time.

'How are you, Ralph?' said Mrs Lambchop. 'Stanley? Say hello to Mr Jones.'

'Take care!' said Mr Jones. 'That balloon is floating – Hmmmm . . . Just where *is* Stanley?'

'Holding the balloon,' Stanley said. 'I got invisible somehow.'

'Is that so? First flat, now invisible.' Ralph Jones shook his head. 'Kids! Always one thing or another, eh, George? My oldest needs dental work. Well, I must run! Say hello to that prince, if he's still visiting. Prince Fawzi Mustafa Aslan Mirza Melek Namerd Haraz, as I recall.'

'A truly *remarkable* memory,' said Mrs Lambchop, as Mr Jones walked away.

By a field in the park, the Lambchops found a bench on which to rest.

On the field, children were racing bicycles, round and round. Suddenly, shouts rose. 'Give up, Billy! Billy's no good! Billy, Billy, silly Billy, he can't ride a bike!'

'That must be Billy,' said Mrs Lambchop.
'The little fellow, so far behind the rest.
Oh, dear! How he teeters!'

Stanley remembered how nervous he
had been when he was learning to ride,
and how his father had steadied him.
Poor Billy! If only – I'll do it! he thought,
and tied his balloon to the bench.

When Billy came round again, Stanley
darted across the field. Taking hold of
the teetering bicycle from behind, he
began to run.

'Uh-oh!' said little Billy, surprised to be gaining speed.

Stanley ran harder, keeping the bicycle steady. The pedals rose and fell, faster and faster, then faster still.

'Yikes!' cried Billy.

Stanley ran as fast as he could.

Soon they passed the boy riding ahead, then another boy, and another! Not until they had passed all the other riders did Stanley, now out of breath, let go.

'Wheeee!' shouted Billy, and went round once more by himself.

'You win, Billy!' shouted the other boys. 'How did you get so good? And so *suddenly*! . . . You sure had us fooled!'

Stanley got his breath back and returned to Mr and Mrs Lambchop on the bench.

'Too bad you missed it, Stanley,' said Mr Lambchop, pretending he had not guessed the truth. 'That teetery little boy, he suddenly rode very well.'

'Oh?' said Stanley, pretending also. 'I wasn't paying attention, I guess.'

Mr Lambchop gave him a little poke in the ribs.

* * *

Half an hour passed, and Mrs Lambchop worried that they might sit too long in the sun. In Stanley's present state, she said, over-tanning would be difficult to detect.

Just then a young man and a pretty girl strolled past, hand in hand, and halted in a grove close by.

'That is Phillip, the son of my dear friend, Mrs Hodgson,' Mrs Lambchop said. 'And the girl must be his sweetheart, Lucia. Such a sad story! They are in love, and Phillip wants very much to propose marriage. But he is too shy. He tries and tries, Mrs Hodgson says, but each time his courage fails. And Lucia is too timid to coax the proposal from him.'

Mr Lambchop was not the least bit shy. 'I'll go introduce myself,' he said. 'And pop the question for him.'

'No, George.' Mrs Lambchop shook her head. 'Lucia must hear the words from his own lips.'

An idea came to Stanley.

'Be right back!' he said, and ran to the grove in which the young couple stood. Beside them, he stood very still.

'. . . nice day, Lucia, don't you think?' Phillip was saying. 'Though they say it may rain. Who knows?'

'You are quite right, I'm sure, Phillip,' the girl replied. 'I do value your opinions about the weather.'

'You are kind, very kind.' Phillip trembled a bit. 'Lucia, I want to ask . . . I mean . . . Would you . . . Consent, that is . . .' He gulped. 'What a pretty dress you have!'

'Thank you,' said Lucia. 'I like your necktie. You were saying, Phillip?'

'Ah!' said Phillip. 'Right! Yes! I want . . .' He bit his lip. 'Look! A dark cloud, there in the west! It may rain after all.'

'I hope not.' Lucia seemed close to tears. 'I mean, if it rained . . .

Well, we might get wet.'

This is *very* boring, Stanley thought.

The conversation grew even more boring. Again and again, Phillip failed to declare his love, chatting instead about the weather, or the look of a tree, or children playing in the park.

'I want to ask, dear Lucia,' Phillip began again, for perhaps the twentieth time, 'if you will ... That is ... If you ... If ...'

'Yes?' said Lucia, for perhaps the twentieth time. '*What*, Phillip? *What* do you wish to say?'

Stanley leaned forward.

'Lucia ... ?' said Phillip. 'Hmmmm ... Ah! I ...'

'*Marry me*!' said Stanley, making his voice as much like Phillip's as he could.

Lucia's eyes opened wide. 'I *will*,

Phillip!' she cried. 'Of course I will marry you!'

Phillip looked as if he might faint. 'What? Did I – ? You *will*?'

Lucia hugged him, and they kissed.

'I've proposed at last!' cried Phillip.
'I can hardly believe I spoke the words!'

You didn't, Stanley thought.

Mr and Mrs Lambchop had seen the lovers embrace. 'Well done, Stanley!' they said when he returned to their bench, and several more times on the way home.

Mrs Hodgson called that evening to report that Phillip and Lucia would soon be wed. 'How wonderful!' Mrs Lambchop said. She had glimpsed them in the park just that afternoon. Such a handsome pair! So much in love!

Stanley teased her. 'You said never to sneak up on people, or spy on them. But I did today. Are you mad at me?'

'Oh, very angry,' said Mrs Lambchop, and kissed the top of his head.

CHAPTER 5
THE TV SHOW

Arthur was feeling left out. 'Stanley always gets to have interesting adventures,' he said. 'And that newspaper story was just about *him*. Nobody seems interested in *me*.'

'The best way to draw attention, dear,' said Mrs Lambchop, 'is by one's character. Be kindly. And fair. Cheerfulness is much admired, as is wit.'

'I can't manage all that,' said Arthur.

Mrs Lambchop spoke privately to Stanley. 'Your brother is a bit jealous,' she said.

'When I was flat, Arthur was jealous because people stared at me,' Stanley said. 'Now they can't see me at all, and he's jealous again.'

Mrs Lambchop sighed. 'If you can find a way to cheer him, do.'

The very next day an important TV person telephoned Mr Lambchop.

'Teddy Talker here, Lambchop,' he said. 'Host of the enormously popular TV chat show, "Talking With Teddy Talker". Will

Stanley appear on it?'

'It would please us to have Stanley *appear* anywhere at all,' Mr Lambchop said. 'People can't see him, you know.'

'I'll just say he's there,' said Teddy Talker. 'Speak to the boy. Let me know.'

Stanley said that he did not particularly care to go on TV. But then he remembered about cheering up Arthur.

'All right,' he said. 'But Arthur too. He likes to tell jokes and do magic tricks. Say we'll *both* be on the show.'

Arthur was very pleased, and that evening the brothers planned what they would do. The next morning, Mr Lambchop told Teddy Talker.

'Excellent plan!' said the TV man. 'This Friday, yes? Thank you, Lambchop!'

'Welcome, everybody!' said Teddy

Talker that Friday evening, from the
stage of his TV theatre. 'Wonderful
guests tonight! Including an invisible boy!'
  In the front row, applauding with

the rest of the audience, Mr and Mrs
Lambchop thought of Stanley and
Arthur, waiting now in a dressing-room
backstage. How excited they must be!

The other guests were already seated on the sofa by Teddy Talker's desk. He chatted first with a lady who had written a book about sausages, then with a tennis champion who had become a rabbi, then with a very pretty young woman who had won a beauty contest, but planned now to devote herself to the cause of world peace. At last came the announcement that began the Lambchop plan.

'Invisible Stanley has been delayed, but will be here shortly,' Teddy Talker told the audience. 'Meanwhile, we are fortunate in having with us his very talented brother!' Protests rose. 'Brother? A *visible* brother? . . . Drat! . . . Good thing we got in free!'

'Ladies and gentlemen!' said Teddy Talker. 'Mirth and Magic with Arthur Lambchop!'

Arthur stepped out on to the stage,

wearing a smart black magician's cape Mrs Lambchop had made for him, and carrying a small box, which he placed on Teddy Talker's desk.

'Hello, everybody!' he said. 'The box is for later. Now let's have fun! Heard the story about the three holes in the ground?' He waited, smiling. 'Well, well, well!'

Two people laughed, but that was all.

'I don't understand,' said a lady sitting behind Mr and Mrs Lambchop.

Mr Lambchop turned in his seat. 'A "well" is a hole in the ground,' he said. '"Well, well, well." Three holes.'

'Ah! I see!' said the lady.

'A riddle, ladies and gentlemen!' cried Arthur. 'Where do kings keep their armies?'

'Where?' someone called.

'In their sleevies!' said Arthur.

Many people laughed now, including the lady who had missed the first joke. 'I *got* that one,' she said.

'And now a mind-reading trick!' Arthur announced. He shuffled a deck of cards, and let Teddy Talker draw one.

'Don't let me see it!' he said. 'But look at it! Picture it in your mind! I will concentrate, using my magic powers!' Arthur closed his eyes. 'Hmmm . . . hmmm . . . Your card, sir, is the four of hearts!'

'It is!' cried Teddy Talker. 'It *is* the four of hearts!'

Voices rose again. 'Incredible! . . . He can read minds? . . . So young, too! . . . Do that one again, lad!'

'Certainly!' said Arthur.

But he had used a false deck in which *every* card was the four of hearts, and the audience would surely guess if that card were named again. Fortunately, the brothers had thought of this. Backstage, Stanley tied his balloon to a chair.

Arthur now shuffled a real deck of cards, then called for a volunteer. When an elderly gentleman came on to the stage, Stanley tiptoed out to stand behind him. The audience applauded the volunteer. How peculiar this is! Stanley thought. Hundreds of people looking, but no one can see me!

'Draw a card, sir!' said Arthur. 'Thank you! Keep it hidden! But picture it in your mind!' Again closing his eyes, he pretended to be thinking hard.

A quick peek told Stanley that the
volunteer held the ten of clubs. Tiptoeing
over, he whispered in his brother's ear.

Arthur opened his eyes. 'I have it. The card is – The ten of clubs!'

'Yes! Bravo!' cried the old gentleman. The audience clapped hard as he returned to his seat.

Mr Lambchop smiled at the lady behind him. 'Our son,' he said.

'So clever!' said the lady. 'What *will* he do next?'

Mrs Lambchop drew a deep breath. That morning, Stanley and Arthur had borrowed a pet frog from the boy next door. What came next, she knew, would be the most daring part of the evening's plan!

'Ladies and gentlemen!'

said Arthur. 'A new kind of magic! Arthur Lambchop – that's me! – and Henry, the Air-Dancing Frog!'

He lifted Henry from the box on Teddy Talker's desk, and held him up. Henry, who appeared to be smiling, wore a little white shirt with an 'H' on it, made by Mrs Lambchop along with Arthur's cape. 'Fly, Henry!' cried Arthur. 'Fly out, and stand still in the air!'

Stepping forward, Stanley took Henry from Arthur's hands and ran to the far side of the stage. Here he stopped, holding the frog high above his head.

Henry wriggled his legs.

'Amazing!' shouted the audience. 'Who'd believe it? . . . That's some frog! . . . What keeps him up there?'

'Circle, Henry!' Arthur commanded. 'Circle in the air!'

Stanley walked rapidly in circles, swaying Henry as he went.

The audience was tremendously impressed. 'What a fine magician! . . . Mind reading *and* frog flying! . . . You don't see that every day!'

Pretending to control Henry's flight, Arthur kept a finger pointed as Stanley swooped the frog all about the stage. 'Whoops!' cried Teddy Talker as Henry flew above his desk. On the long sofa, the sausage writer and tennis rabbi and the beauty contest winner ducked down.

Even Mr and Mrs Lambchop, knowing the secret of Henry's flight, thought it an amazing sight.

At last, to great applause, Arthur took Henry into his own hands and returned him to the little box.

Stanley tiptoed off to get his smiley-face balloon. The plan now called for Teddy Talker to announce the arrival of the invisible boy, and introduce him.

But Arthur had stepped forward again.

'Thank you for cheering me,' he told the audience. 'But I have to say something. That first mind-reading trick, I really did do that one. But the second trick – Actually, I can't read minds at all. And the flying frog, he –'

Voices rose. 'Can't read minds? . . . We've been lied to! . . . The *frog* was lying? . . . Not the frog, stupid! . . . Wait, he's not done!'

'Please! Listen!' said Arthur. 'It wouldn't be fair to let you think I did everything by myself. I had a helper! The second trick, he saw the card and told me what it was. And Henry . . . Well, my helper was whooshing him in the air!'

By now the audience was terribly confused. 'Who? . . . What helper? . . . It was just a regular frog? . . . But *some* frogs fly! . . . No, squirrels, not frogs! . . . *Whooshing*?'

Arthur went on. 'My brother Stanley helped me! He fixed it for me to be on this show! He's a really nice brother, and I thank him a lot!'

Teddy Talker had sprung to his feet. 'Ladies and gentlemen! May I present now a very special guest, who has been here all along! The invisible boy! Stanley Lambchop!'

Stanley came on to the stage, carrying his smiley-face balloon. Arthur put out his hand, and the audience could tell that Stanley had taken it. There was tremendous applause.

The brothers bowed again and again, Stanley's balloon bobbing up and down. Arthur's smile was plain to see, and Mr and Mrs Lambchop, as they applauded, thought that even the balloon's painted smile seemed brighter than before.

'I have two children myself,' said the lady behind them. 'Both entirely visible, and without theatrical flair. We are a very *usual* family.'

'As we are,' said Mr Lambchop, smiling. 'Mostly, that is.'

Arthur left the stage, and Stanley sat on the sofa between the sausage writer and the beauty contest winner and answered Teddy Talker's questions. He had no idea *how* he became invisible, he said, and it wasn't actually a great treat being that way, since he often got bumped into, and had to keep reminding people he was there. After that, Teddy Talker thanked everyone for coming, and the show was over.

Back home, Arthur felt the evening had gone well.

'I got lots of applause,' he said. 'But maybe it was mostly because of what Stanley did. I shouldn't be too proud, I guess.'

'Poise and good humour contribute greatly to a performer's success,' said Mrs Lambchop. 'You did well on both those counts. Return Henry in the morning, dear. Time now for bed.'

CHAPTER 6
THE BANK ROBBERS

Mr Lambchop and Stanley and Arthur were watching the evening news on TV.

'. . . more dreadful scandal and violence tomorrow,' said the newscaster, ending a report on national affairs. 'Here in our fair city, another bank was robbed today, the third this month. The unusual robbers –'

'Enough of crime!' Bustling in, Mrs Lambchop switched off the TV. 'Come to dinner!'

Stanley supposed he would never know how the robbers were unusual. But the next afternoon, while strolling with Mr Lambchop, he found out. On the way home they passed a bank.

'I must cash a cheque, but it is very crowded in there,' said Mr Lambchop. 'Wait here, Stanley.'

Stanley waited.

Suddenly cries rose from within the bank. 'Lady bank robbers! Just like they said on TV! I laughed when I heard it! . . . Me too!'

Two women in dresses and fancy hats, one stout and the other very tall, ran out of the bank, each with a moneybag in one hand and a pistol in the other.

'Stay in there!' the stout woman called back into the bank, her voice high and

scratchy. 'Don't anyone run out! Or else . . .
Bang! Bang!'

'Right!' shouted the tall woman, also in an odd, high voice.

'Just because we are females doesn't mean we can't shoot!'

Being invisible won't protect me if bullets go flying about! Stanley thought. He looked for a place to hide.

An empty Yum-Yum Ice-Cream van was parked close by, and he jumped into it. His balloon still floated outside the van, its string caught in the door, but he did not dare to rescue it. Scrunching down behind cardboard barrels marked 'Yum Chocolate', 'Strawberry Yum', and 'Yum Crunch', he peeked out.

An alarm was ringing inside the bank, and now shouts rose again. 'Ha! Now you're in trouble! The police will come! . . .

Put that money back where you found it, ladies!'

Then Stanley saw that the two robber women were running towards him, carrying their money bags. They were stopping! They were getting into the Yum-Yum van!

Scrunching down again, he held his breath.

The robbers were in the van, close by where he hid. 'Hurry up!' said the stout woman, in a surprisingly deep voice. 'These shoes are killing me!'

The tall woman opened the 'Yum Crunch' barrel, and Stanley saw that it was empty. Then both robbers poured packets of money from their bags into the barrel, and put the lid back on again.

Stanley could hardly believe what he saw next!

The robbers threw aside their fancy hats, and tugged off wigs! And now they were undressing, pulling their dresses over their heads!

They were *men*, Stanley realised, not women! Yes! Underneath the dresses they wore white ice-cream-man pants, with the legs rolled up, and white Yum Yum shirts!

'Whew! What a relief, Howard!' The stout robber kicked off his women's shoes, and put on white sneakers.

'They'll never catch us now, Ralph!' said the tall one.

The robbers unrolled their trouser legs and threw their female clothing into another empty barrel, the one marked 'Yum Chocolate'. Then they jumped into the front seats, the tall man driving, and the van sped off.

Behind the barrels, Stanley held his breath again. The pair was too clever to be caught! They were sure to get away! No one would suspect two Yum-Yum men of being lady – But the van was slowing! It was stopping.

Stanley peeked out again.

A police car blocked the road, and two policemen stood beside it, inspecting cars as they passed by. In a moment, they were at the Yum-Yum van.

'A bank got robbed,' the first policeman told the driver. 'By two women. You ice-cream fellows seen any suspicious looking females?'

'My!' The tall man shook his head. 'More and more these days, women filling roles once played by men. Bless 'em I say!'

Beside him, the stout man said hastily, 'But bank robbing, Howard, that's *wrong*.'

The second policeman looked into the back of the van. 'Just ice-cream here,' he told his partner.

The trickery is working! Stanley thought. How can I –? An idea came to him. Reaching out, he flipped the lid off the 'Yum Chocolate' barrel.

'Loose lid,' said the second policeman. 'Better tighten – Hey! This barrel is full of female clothes!'

'Oh!' The tall robber made a sad face. 'For the needy,' he said. 'They were my late mother's.'

Stanley flipped the the lid off the 'Yum Crunch' barrel, and the packets of money were plain to see!

'Your mother was a mighty rich woman!' shouted the first policeman, drawing his pistol. 'Hands up, you two!'

As the robbers were being handcuffed,
another police car drove up. Mr
Lambchop jumped out of it.

'That balloon, on that van!' he shouted. 'We've been following it! Stanley? . . . Are you in there?'

'Yes!' Stanley called back. 'I'm fine. The bank robbers are caught! They weren't ladies at all, just dressed that way!'

The handcuffed robbers were dreadfully confused. 'Who's yelling in our van? . . . Who stuck a balloon in the door? . . . Have we gone crazy?' they said.

'It's my son, Stanley,' said Mr Lambchop. 'He is invisible, unfortunately. Thank goodness he was not hurt!'

'That must be the same invisible boy they had on TV!' said the first policeman.

'An invisible boy?' The tall robber groaned. 'After all my careful planning!'

The stout robber shrugged. 'You can't

68

think of everything, Howard. Don't blame yourself.'

The robbers were driven off to jail, and Stanley went home with Mr Lambchop in a cab.

Stanley had been far too brave, Mrs Lambchop said when she heard what he had done. Really! Flipping those ice-cream lids! Arthur said he'd have flipped them too, if he'd thought of it.

CHAPTER 7
ARTHUR'S STORM

Mr and Mrs Lambchop had said goodnight. For a moment the brothers lay silent in their beds.

Then Arthur yawned. 'Goodnight, Stanley. Pleasant dreams.'

'Pleasant dreams? Hah!'

'Hah?'

'Those robbers today, they had *guns*!' said Stanley. 'I could have got shot by accident, and nobody would even know.'

'I never thought of that.' Arthur sat up.
'Are you mad at me?'

'I guess not. But . . .' Stanley sighed.
'The thing is, I don't want to go on being
invisible. I was really scared today, and I
hate carrying that balloon, but when I
don't people bump into me. And I can't

see myself in the mirror, so I don't even remember how I look! It's like when I was flat. It was all right for a while, but then people laughed at me.'

'That's why I blew you round again,' Arthur said proudly. 'Everyone said how smart I was.'

'If you're so smart, get me out of *this* fix!' There was a little tremble in Stanley's voice.

Arthur went to sit on the edge of his brother's bed. Feeling for a foot beneath the covers, he patted it. 'I'm really sorry for you,' he said. 'I wish –'

There was a knock at the door, and Mr and Mrs Lambchop came in. 'Talking, you two? You ought to be asleep,' they said.

Arthur explained about Stanley's unhappiness.

'There's more,' Stanley said. 'Twice my friends had parties, and didn't invite me. They forget me sometimes even if I *do* keep waving that balloon!'

'Poor dear!' Mrs Lambchop said. '"Out of sight, out of mind," as the saying goes.' She went to put her arms around Stanley, but he had just sat up in bed, and she missed him. She found him and gave him a hug.

'This is awful!' Arthur said. 'We have to *do* something!'

Mr Lambchop shook his head. 'Doctor Dan knew of no cure for Stanley's condition. And little about its cause, except for a possible connection between bad weather and fruit.'

'Then I'll always be like this.' Stanley's voice trembled again. 'I'll get older and bigger, but no one will ever see.'

Arthur was thinking. 'Stanley did eat fruit. And there *was* a storm. Maybe – Wait!'

He explained his idea.

Mr and Mrs Lambchop looked at each other, then at where they supposed Stanley to be, and at each other again.

'I'm not afraid,' said Stanley. 'Let's *try*!'

Mr Lambchop nodded. 'I see no harm in it.'

'Nor I,' said Mrs Lambchop. 'Very well, Arthur! Let us gather what your plan requires!'

'Everyone ready?' said Arthur. 'It has to be just the way it was the night Stanley got invisible.'

'I'm wearing the same blue-and-white

stripey pyjamas,' said Stanley. 'And I have an apple. And a box of raisins.'

'We can't make a real storm,' Arthur said. 'But maybe this will work.'

He stepped into the bathroom and ran the water in the basin and shower. 'There's rain,' he said, returning. 'I'll be wind.'

Mrs Lambchop held up a wooden spoon and a large frying-pan from her kitchen. 'Thunder ready,' she said.

Mr Lambchop showed the powerful torch he had fetched from his tool kit. 'Lightning ready.'

Stanley raised his apple. 'Now?'

'Go stand by the window,' said Arthur. 'Now let me think. Hmmm . . . It was dark.' He put out the light. 'Go on, eat. *Whooosh*!' he added, being wind.

Stanley began to eat the apple.

Water pattered down in the bathroom, into the basin and from the shower into the bathtub.

'*Whooosh . . . whooosh*!' said Arthur, and Mrs Lambchop struck her frying-pan with the wooden spoon. The *crash!* was much like thunder.

'Lightning, please,' Arthur said.

Mr Lambchop aimed his torch and flicked it on and off while Stanley finished the apple.

'Now the raisins,' said Arthur. 'One at a time. *Whooosh*!'

Stanley opened the little box and ate a raisin. Still *whooshing*, Arthur conducted as if an orchestra sat before him. His left hand signalled Mrs Lambchop to strike the frying pan, the

right one Mr Lambchop to flash the light.
Nods told Stanley when to eat a raisin.

Patter . . . splash . . . went the water
in the bathroom. *Whooosh!* went Arthur.
Crash! went the frying-pan. *Flash! . . .
flash!* went the light.

'If anyone should see us now,' Mrs
Lambchop said softly, 'I should be hard
put to explain.' Stanley looked down at
himself. 'It's no use,' he said. 'I'm still
invisible.'

'Twist around!' said Arthur. 'Maybe the
noise and light have to hit you just a
certain way!'

Twisting, Stanley ate three more
raisins. The light flickered over him.
He heard the water splashing, Arthur
whoooshing, the pounding of the frying-
pan by the spoon. How hard they were

trying, he thought. How much he loved them all!

But he was still invisible.

'There's only one raisin left,' he said. 'It's no use.'

'Poor Stanley!' cried Mrs Lambchop.

Arthur could not bear the thought of never seeing his brother again. 'Do the last raisin, Stanley,' he said. 'Do it!'

Stanley ate the raisin, and did one more twist. Mrs Lambchop tapped her frying-pan and Mr Lambchop flashed his light. Arthur gave a last *whooosh*!

Nothing happened.

'At least I'm not hungry,' Stanley said bravely. 'But –' He put a hand to his cheek. 'I feel . . . Sort of tingly.'

'Stanley!' said Mr Lambchop. 'Are you touching your cheek? I see your hand,

I think!'

'And your pyjamas!' shouted Arthur, switching on the light.

A sort of outline of Stanley Lambchop, with hazy stripes running up and down it, had appeared by the window. Through the stripes, they could see the house next door.

Suddenly, the outline filled in. There stood Stanley in his striped pyjamas, just as they remembered him!

'I can see my feet!' Stanley shouted. 'It's *me*!'

'"*I*," dear, not "me!",' said Mrs Lambchop before she could catch herself, then ran to hold him tight.

Mr Lambchop shook hands with Arthur, and then they all went into the bathroom to watch Stanley look at himself in the mirror. It hadn't mattered when he was invisible, Mrs Lambchop said, but he was greatly in need of a haircut now.

She made hot chocolate to celebrate the occasion, and Arthur's cleverness was acknowledged by all.

'But false storms cannot be relied upon,' Mr Lambchop said. 'We must think twice before eating fruit during bad weather. Especially by a window.'

Then the brothers were tucked into bed again. 'Goodnight,' said Mr and Mrs Lambchop, putting out the light.

'Goodnight,' said Stanley and Arthur.

Stanley got up and went to have another look in the bathroom mirror. 'Thank you, Arthur,' he said, returning. 'You saved me from being flat, and now you've saved me again.'

'Oh, well . . .' Arthur yawned. 'Stanley?
Try to stay, you know, regular for a
while.'

'I will,' said Stanley.

Soon they were both asleep.

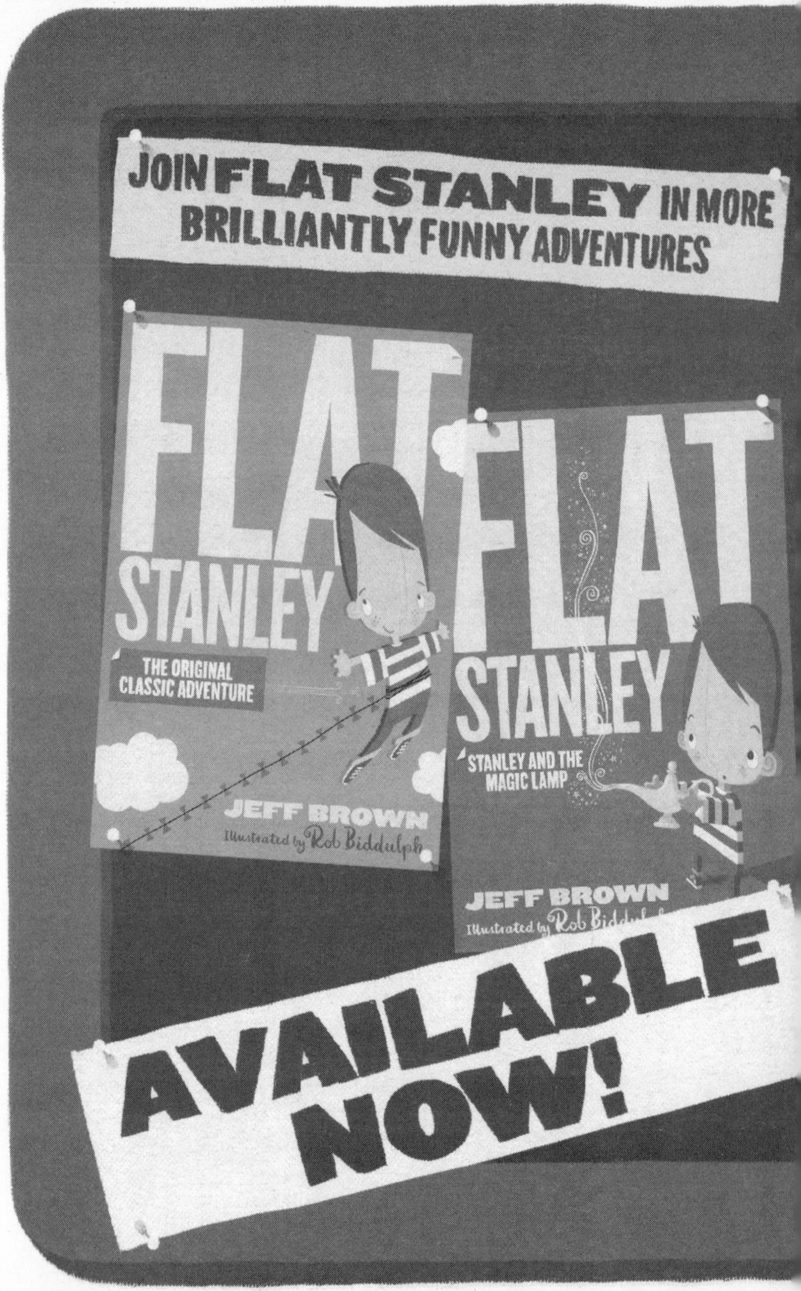
JOIN FLAT STANLEY IN MORE
BRILLIANTLY FUNNY ADVENTURES
FLAT STANLEY
THE ORIGINAL CLASSIC ADVENTURE
JEFF BROWN
Illustrated by Rob Biddulph
FLAT STANLEY
STANLEY AND THE MAGIC LAMP
JEFF BROWN
AVAILABLE NOW!

Farshore

Amazing things
always happen
to Stanley!

FLAT
STANLEY

INVISIBLE
STANLEY

JEFF BROWN
Illustrated by Rob Biddulph

FLAT
STANLEY

STANLEY'S CHRISTMAS
ADVENTURE

JEFF BROWN
Illustrated by Rob Biddulph